The Kingdom of Broken Magic

The Kingdom of Broken Magic

Christine Aziz

Illustrations by Ewa Beniak–Haremska

EVERYTHING WITH WORDS

Published in the UK in 2023 by Everything with Words Limited,
Fifth Floor, 30–31 Furnival Street, London EC4A 1JQ

www.everythingwithwords.com

Printed and bound in Great Britain by CPI Group (UK) Ltd,
Croydon CRO 4YY

A CIP catalogue record for this book is available
from the British Library.

ISBN 978-1-911427-308

For Alan Gartland 1959–2022

1

Maggie opened her eyes to the cold, damp morning. It was the beginning of everything. Unaware of the day's significance, she raised her head from a pile of rags and scanned the attic. Everything was as it always was: pigeon poo dripped through the roof, bats rustled in the rafters and tiny paws scuttled across the floor. She burrowed back into the rags hoping the day would disappear, but something, or someone, tickled her toes.

"Leave me alone," she groaned, pushing whatever, or whoever it was away with her foot.

An urgent voice echoed through the attic, "Wake up, Maggie. We're late. If we don't go down now, you know what'll happen to us."

Maggie looked up and scowled at the small boy offering her his hand.

"How can you be so bright and early?" she said as Josh hauled her up from the rags.

"Dunno," he said, grinning and tugging fingers through matted curls. "Better hurry."

They moved towards the stairs but stopped as an icy chill settled around them and the slow, deliberate flapping of wings filled the stairwell. A black crow flew into the attic stirring tiny whirls of dust from the floorboards. It circled above their heads ignoring their efforts to shoo it away. Drawing closer, it settled its wiry talons on Maggie's head.

"Ouch go away. You're hurting me," she said, trying to shake the bird off, but its talons only dug deeper into her scalp. It looked down its black beak and squawked, "Downstairs!"

"Get off her," Josh said, pulling at its wings. A woman's voice rose from several floors below.

"Carry-On! Get down here. Quick!"

The crow rose in the air, strands of Maggie's hair falling from its talons, and flew out of the attic with a low, guttural caw.

Maggie turned crossly to Josh, small beads of blood blossoming in her hair.

"I can look after myself, thank you," she said, folding her arms firmly across her chest.

"Nice to have a bit of help though," Josh said, and, grinning, added, "Carry-On suits you as a hat."

Maggie punched him affectionately and laughed. She did not know if she had a brother, but if she did, she was sure he would look like Josh. And if he had a sister, which he might, somewhere, Josh thought she would look like Maggie. They shared the same dark complexion, eyes and hair. Maggie always chopped hers into short spikes, while Josh let his corkscrew crazily over his shoulders. Dark circles framed their eyes, and their skin was covered in scabs, bruises and sores which they constantly picked at.

Josh looked around at the puddles of water seeping into the piles of rags which served as their beds.

"I hate this place," he said. "It would be even worse without you, Mags."

Maggie gave what she hoped was a comforting smile, but which hid the same fearful thought – what would she do without Josh? He was her only friend and ally at the Scribbens' Home for Very Wayward Children. They knew nothing else and were each other's family. All they knew was that they had either been dumped on the Home's doorstep or dropped down its coal chute as babies.

Maggie wrinkled her soot-smudged nose. "You smell, Josh."

"So do you!"

Maggie smiled and waved a hand in the air graciously like royalty. "Yes, like a rose."

Josh sniffed at the air. "Mmmm… sausages and mash, pies and gravy…"

They giggled and their mouths watered.

"Let's run away," Josh said. "We can make a dash for it when the gate's opened."

"Again? They always find us."

"We might be lucky this time."

They had run away so many times, they had lost count. Each time they were caught and dragged back to the Home and punished.

A louse crawled from Josh's grimy collar and headed for his chin. Maggie shot a hand out, pincered it between her fingers and popped it.

"Four," she said.

Josh flicked a louse from Maggie's arm to the floor and squashed it with a bare foot. "Six. I'm winning," he said. Their laughter was interrupted by the woman calling again from downstairs.

Maggie clutched at Josh's hand. "I can't stand it anymore. Every day I wake up and wish it was my last day here," she said, holding back tears.

"Promise you won't go anywhere without me, Mags."

"I promise. We'll always be together, Josh," Maggie said as they rushed out of the room.

An enormous woman squatted on the bottom of the stairs in a large feathered hat. She levered herself up with the help of the bannisters and turned a face like uncooked pastry towards them. Maggie and Josh instantly wished they had a rolling pin to flatten Miss Scribbens into a pie crust.

"What do you say to your one and only?" she crooned.

"Good morning, Miss Scribbens," they chorused.

"Very good," she said, herding them towards the kitchen, her feet slapping behind them like wet fish. Her long, full skirt scraped against the walls. It was stitched with pockets full of "things-that-might-come-in-handy", such as candles, spanners, screws, stockings, slippers, walnuts, boiled sweets, a compass and bread and cheese. Carry-On flew down, plucked a dead mouse from one of them and settled on her shoulders. Cries of babies rose from the basement.

"You're late again," Miss Scribbens said in a voice strangled by the many jewelled necklaces fastened tightly around her neck. "Lateness is thievery. Stealing time, but you're good at stealing. You're the bestest pickpocket we've

had, Miss Fever Fingers. But remember, you must never disappoint your one and only, who wants gold coins. Lots of them."

"Gold. Gold. Gold," Carry-On crowed, chewing on its mouse.

"Remember you are Wayward and Wayward is what the Devil does," Miss Scribbens said. "Which is why nobody wants you, except your dear, kind Miss Scribbens."

All around them, the Home's massive rooms and long dark corridors filled with the sounds of small hands dusting and polishing. A tiny girl moved slowly past the door on her hands and knees, scrubbing at the stone floor. Carry-On flew towards her with a creaky triumphant caw and tipped her bucket over. A stream of soapy water poured down the long corridor. Trembling, the girl stood up, her skirt soaked.

Miss Scribbens thrust a large bag into Maggie's hand.

"You can never escape your Miss Scribbens. Carry-On and his birdy mates have an eye on every street corner."

The crow pecked viciously at Maggie's heels, propelling her towards the back door. Miss Scribbens pushed Josh through the kitchen and into the scullery.

"Wash the dishes, and if I catch you licking the plates again, you know what will happen."

A heavily ringed hand shot before him. Josh shivered. With a loud laugh she threw some plates into the sink, turned on the tap and squeezed herself out of the door.

Josh stared through the window at the yard disappearing into a foul stew of creeping fog. The Home's iron gates clanged shut, and Maggie's muffled footsteps grew fainter. Josh felt suddenly afraid. Would he ever see her again?

2

The fog's filthy fingers reached into Maggie's throat as she groped her way through a series of dank archways into a street of expensive shops. Ghostly figures passed her by, coughing and spluttering. Carriages and horses nudged the kerb, their wheels and hooves muffled by the fog. She

glimpsed a woman, as if through a veil, hurrying her child along, an arm wrapped protectively around his shoulders. Maggie sighed wistfully as she imagined them arriving at their home welcomed by warmth and laughter. She and Josh both longed to be part of a family, but in their hearts they knew it would never happen. Who would want two smelly, lice-ridden children? They were doomed to be at the Scribbens' Home forever. Maggie tried not to feel sorry for herself as the fog thickened around her. Perfect for pickpocketing. Soon, she was bumping into passers-by and apologising while invisibly removing coins, wallets, snuff boxes, fobs, purses, brooches, tie pins, cuff links, gold cigarette cases, with quick, light fingers.

Her bag grew heavy. Tired and weak with hunger, she collapsed into a doorway. Just one more picked pocket before I rest, she thought. She heard the steady tap of a stick on the pavement and watched as a short man, round as a plum, emerged from the thinning fog. He wore a thick red cloak and twirled an ebony cane in one hand. His silver preened moustache curled like a question mark around his cheeks.

Maggie held out her hand. "Please sir."

He smiled kindly and searched through his pockets.

Maggie's eyes flicked over his fur-lined cloak and the jacket beneath it. He stared down at her bare feet.

"You must be freezing, child," he said. "Where do you live?"

Maggie sniffled. Concerned, the man leant towards her, and she smelt spices and tobacco. Her fingers darted into his pockets like arrows. She clasped something that felt like a small stone. A jewel perhaps? The man seized her wrist and looked disappointed. "Foolish child," he said.

Maggie sank her teeth into his hand and ran as fast as she could, the stone clasped tightly in her hand.

"Thief, thief!" the man cried as he ran after her. Others joined him. The bag slowed her down. Turning it upside down, she emptied its contents across the cobbles. People fought over its spilt treasure, blocking her pursuer's path. The stone grew hot in her hand, burning her palm. Her legs grew weak, and her chest ached. The fog thinned, and she saw the man still running behind her with a policeman who waved a truncheon and blew his whistle at her. If they caught her, she would be thrown into prison, or worse, returned to the Home. She sprinted forwards but a large crowd of cheering people formed a solid wall against her. There was no escape.

The policeman reached out to grab Maggie. She dived into the crowd and disappeared through a forest of legs. She reached the kerb and stood up. The crowd pushed and shoved behind her as clowns on unicycles juggled dinner sets, and acrobats turned giddying circles They gasped in horror as the shadow of a huge grey beast loomed above them. A strange long nose hung like a snake from between its tiny eyes and plucked hats from heads and sent them spinning into the air. A fire-eater balanced on the creature's back, a blaze of flames shooting from his mouth. Children tugged at the creature's brightly knitted scarf and gasped when it twined its nose around a small boy and lifted him onto its head. Ladies fainted at the sight of its enormous bottom.

"The circus! The circus!" the children cried, but fell silent as a large cage rolled slowly past them. The crowd shrank back. Three of the biggest cats Maggie had ever seen peered through the bars at the crowds. They growled and roared, revealing long, sharp teeth. One of them chewed on a large bone.

A caravan, painted in all the colours of the rainbow, trundled behind them. Music tinkled from its windows and blue smoke rose from its tiny chimney. The crowd surged forwards. Maggie gave a loud scream and fell into

the street. She watched helplessly as the caravan's iron wheels crunched steadily towards her.

A sudden rush of air lifted Maggie from the ground and a pair of feathered arms pulled her through the caravan window.

"Here you are dearie, home at last," a woman's voice soothed as the arms folded around her like a pair of giant wings. Maggie stared up at the bright apparition that held her so tightly. Eyes as bright as a summer sky were shuttered by purple-painted lids, a tiara swayed from a stiff mountain of orange hair and her lips blazed red. Maggie blinked – she had never seen so much colour on one person.

The stranger set her down, revealing the full effect of the blue and silver satin corset. A tiny skirt covered the tops of the woman's muscled legs. "My own dear one, fate has delivered you into my arms. I have been looking for a child like you for a very long time. You're the right size, the right shape, the right everything," the woman said, her eyes puddled with tears.

Maggie swayed on the caravan's travelling floor and gawped.

"Do you want to go back to where you came from? I'm not a kidnapper. I won't keep you against your will."

The delicious smell of apple pie and gammon wafted

from a small burning range. The woman looked fondly at her. "I noticed you before you fell and thought how perfect you were. Perfect. Of course, you had to be rescued when you fell, but I would have taken you anyway. What else was I to do?"

She whirled around, and Maggie had the impression of fireworks going off. The air thickened like a swarm of bees and the caravan spun around her.

"Who are you?" she asked.

"I am the spectacular, audacious, miraculous, breath-taking, one-and-only Flying Lulu – the bestest trapeze artiste in the world. You, dear child, can call me Madam Lulu. I shall be your new mistress and shall dedicate my life to teaching you the art of dancing in the air as if you were a bird."

"A bird?"

"Of course. I am THE STAR of the one and only Mrs Gumbo's Flying Circus," she said and stared at Maggie with glittering eyes. "What is your name, dear child?

"Maggie."

15

Madam Lulu smiled, "I like you Maggie and I will like you even better if you can dance."

The caravan shook as Maggie skipped, hopped and waved her arms to Madam Lulu's tuneless singing.

"How can you have such small feet and long legs and move like a slug in treacle?" Madam Lulu cried as if she had made a terrible mistake. She placed a coin upon the floor and instructed Maggie to cover the coin with the tips of her toes and to spin like a top.

Maggie looked down at her bare, grimy feet and lifted herself onto her toes. She flapped her arms but her toes hurt, and she lost her balance. Disappointed, Madam Lulu gave her a long thin stick to hold. "Curl your hands around this and grip it tightly. Do NOT let go no matter how hard I pull."

Maggie gripped the baton as if her life depended upon it. Madam Lulu pulled and pulled, but could not prise the baton from her. She twirled Maggie around faster and faster until Maggie thought she would be sick. Madam Lulu was pleased.

"Very well done. But... can you fly?"

"Fly? I don't know, not having had the mind to try."

"Try, dearie. Nothing is gained without trying. Flap

your arms. Like this." Madam Lulu flapped her muscled arms and rose from the floor. She spun so fast that the air grew hot, whirled and sucked pictures from the walls. Maggie's eyes popped from their sockets.

"Your turn," Madam Lulu said, slowing to a halt.

Maggie flapped her arms, but her feet remained fixed to the travelling floor.

"You are very weak. You must eat."

Maggie felt a sharp pang and moved towards the door.

"Can I bring my mate Josh? He's hungry too."

"Oh no, I cannot be doing with two of you. One does very nicely, thank you."

"But Josh will be cross. I promised I would never leave him alone at the Home."

"He'll soon forget you. Boys always do."

"I'm sorry Madam Lulu," she said, "but I can't stay. I have to go back to Josh."

Maggie moved closer to the door. Succulent smells pulled at her like reins on a horse. She struggled with the door handle.

*

Maggie woke to the sound of Madam Lulu's out-of-tune humming, and the smell of toast, egg and brewed tea. She

17

sat up and groaned. How could she have forgotten Josh so quickly? She had only intended to stay for dinner, but afterwards, Madam Lulu had bathed her in hot soapy water and dressed her in a lavender-scented nightgown. A tiny bed was pulled down from the caravan wall and she had sunk into its feathered softness. For the first time in her life she had fallen asleep without hunger gnawing at her belly, but it had been replaced with guilt. The thought of Josh shivering alone on the attic floor forced her out of bed.

"Where are my clothes?" she cried. "I have to get back to Josh."

Madam Lulu wrinkled her nose.

"I burnt them. Filthy things. Crawling with lice." She eyed Maggie's hair, "I'm sure your hair is crawling with them. I shall de-lice you today."

"I've got nothing to wear now."

Madam Lulu handed her a tray of hot buttered toast, marmalade, fried eggs and sweet tea.

"Nothing can be done on an empty stomach."

Madam Lulu was right. Maggie piled marmalade onto her toast and topped it with an egg while recounting her life with Josh at the Scribbens' Home for Very Wayward Children.

Madam Lulu pulled a big red handkerchief from her bodice and held it to her eyes. "You can't go back to that dreadful place."

"But I have to get Josh out. He can't stay there."

"Of course, but you must be clever about it and not rush into anything. Miss Scribbens is a cunning woman. Things often have a way of sorting themselves out if you leave them alone. But sometimes you need a Plan."

"I've never had a Plan before. We don't have much use for them at the Home."

Madam Lulu blew her nose and sniffed. "First, we must let Josh know you are safe."

"How?"

"I shall help you to write a letter to Josh and have it delivered in secret."

Maggie gobbled up another egg and sipped noisily at her tea. She burped and lay back against her pillows.

"I'll stay," she said. "And when I'm strong enough I'll go back for Josh."

Madam Lulu clapped her hands joyfully and hugged her.

"I shall make you a STAR of the circus! I need someone to take over from me now that I'm getting old," she said and pulled out a dull round stone from her pocket. "Oh dear, in all the excitement, I forgot this. It fell from your clothes."

"It's the gentleman's jewel," Maggie cried.

"Hardly a jewel," Madam Lulu said. "But you should keep it. It might bring you luck."

"It doesn't even shine."

"The plainest of things often prove to be the most valuable of all."

Maggie stared at the black stone in her hand. There was nothing special about it, apart from a thin orange line running around it like a thread.

"I stole it."

"Then borrow it, until you find the owner and can return it."

Madam Lulu opened a cupboard and held up a dress.

"It was Fozia's. It's yours now."

"Who's Fozia?"

Miss Lulu pulled out her handkerchief again and wiped her eyes.

"I was teaching her to be an aerialist. But tragedy struck…"

"What happened?"

Madam Lulu wailed loudly. "No one knows what happened to her. She just disappeared into thin air."

3

The circus stopped for the night in a field. Maggie peered from the caravan door. Three huge tigers lazed upon the grass, chins resting on their paws, lazily flicking their tails over the grass. Their marked orange fur burned like fire in the twilight. A short, round man with long black hair and eyelashes that fluttered like insect wings shouted at them.

"Clench your stomach muscles, gals. Squeeze, squeeze. Now release."

One of the tigers groaned and rolled over. The man tapped her with a whip.

"Rara, how on earth do you think you can wear a bolero if you don't hold that stomach in," he said.

"For goodness sake, Jeffrey. Are you trying to kill me?" Rara said.

"Daaaahling, you'd make a lovely rug if he did," drawled Dewi, the smallest and sleekest of the tigers.

"You're unusually sharp this evening, Dewi," Citra said, turning to Rara for a response. The largest of the three tigers nodded sleepily.

Jeffrey cracked his whip angrily.

"You're supposed to be tigers not kittens!" he yelled.

"Keep it down, Jeffrey. We're a bit delicate today. We were partying all last night," Citra said, yawning and struggling to sit up on her hind legs.

"Partying?" screamed Jeffrey.

Rara yawned. "It was wild."

"That new monkey is hilarious," Citra said. "His juggling's not bad, either."

Jeffrey threw his whip at them.

"If you don't exercise you won't be MEAN and LEAN like tigers are supposed to be."

The trio smiled at each other. "C'mon Dewi. Get meeeeeeeean and leeeeeean, honey," Citra purred.

Rara winked at Maggie. "Hey little girl, come over here and give my tummy a tickle."

Maggie hesitated. Jeffrey pushed her forwards. "They won't hurt you. UN-fortunately."

Maggie pushed her hands into Rara's soft, thick fur.

The tiger squealed with delight and waved her long sharp claws in the air. Jeffrey buried his head in his hands.

"The man who sold me them said they were vicious Sumatran tigers," he wailed. "They snarled, roared, got their claws out. Their eyes blazed. I thought they would eat me alive. So, I bought them. Three for ten guineas. It seemed a good deal at the time. But when we got home, all they did was sleep and purr."

Rara slipped a paw round Maggie's waist.

"They're harmless and worthless," Jeffrey said. "All they want to do is party."

Maggie fidgeted in her dress. She wasn't used to collars and cuffs and kept tripping over its hem and petticoats. The shoes were worse. Her feet felt like birds in a cage. Rara tugged at her sleeve. "You're wearing Fozia's dress. It suits you. A perfect fit."

"What happened to her?" Maggie said.

The tigers froze. Jeffrey paled.

"No-one talks about the folk gone missing. It's dangerous," Dewi said.

Citra sniffed at Maggie's hair. "You're as pretty as a sweet pea."

Maggie blushed. "You have such beautiful coats," she said, stroking Rara's shining fur.

"It's boring wearing the same coat year in and year out, darling," Citra grumbled.

"At least our music is better than yours," Rara said.

"What's tiger music like?"

"Tuneless caterwauling about jungles and stuff," Jeffrey said.

"You sing?"

"Let's show her, girls," Rara said.

The tigers jumped up. They swayed their hips and beat out a rhythm with their tails. Their voices pulsed with drums, birdsong, pipes and bells as they sang of jungles, blossoms and juicy fruits. The air grew damp and warm, and Maggie's nose filled with the perfume of exotic flowers. She jumped up to join them, shaking her hips and jumping up and down with a joy that was as strange and new to her as a jungle.

Madam Lulu came running over to them and clapped her hands.

"You don't have time for this," she said, pulling Maggie from the singing tigers towards a small striped tent. "No time for play. Tomorrow will be your first training day and soon you'll be performing in the Big Top!"

Maggie blew the tigers a kiss, unaware that by the end of the next day her hands would burn, her body ache and

25

her feet blister. She was used to keeping her feet firmly on the ground, passing her hands like quicksilver through pockets and running off at top speed; but above the ground, gripping trapeze bars, balancing on high wires, climbing ropes, she was lost. For hours on end she repeated Madam Lulu's exercises to build up her strength, balance and flexibility.

"Your legs are strong, but you must work on your grip, arm and shoulder strength," Madam Lulu said as Maggie cartwheeled her way around the caravan. "There is also the matter of concentration. It's dangerous to lose it, even for a second."

At the end of each day Madam Lulu rubbed herbal creams into Maggie's aching body.

"I've got muscles I didn't know I had," she groaned, wincing as Madam Lulu massaged her bruised feet. Her eyes ached with the strain of judging aerial distance and speed, and the backs of her knees were sore from hanging from trapeze bars. She lay back, exhausted.

"I can't do this! It's too hard."

"Don't be ridiculous. You're a natural," Madam Lulu said, vigorously pounding her shins.

"Ouch," howled Maggie.

"How did you feel when you flew through the hoop today from one trapeze to another?"

Maggie recalled the exhilarating rush as she let go of the trapeze bar and projected her body forwards into mid-air. "Like a bird. Free," she said, and thought how flying through the air without a safety net felt safer than being a pickpocket in a city's mean and unforgiving streets.

Madam Lulu clapped her hands in delight. "You shall fly around the Big Top like a meteorite. The audience will rise to their feet and clap until their hands drop off! In one day you have progressed beyond my wildest dreams."

Maggie's eyes widened. She had only ever been praised for her pickpocketing, but never for anything else. "Do you really think I shall be able to fly like a bird, Madam?"

"Of course, but we must keep rehearsing. Practice makes perfect."

There was so much to learn, Madam Lulu explained: techniques for both flying and static trapeze as well as innumerable rope manoeuvres such as the Meat Drop Climb and the more complicated Curly Wurly. She dragged books from cupboards and showed her illustrations of countless above-ground acrobatic moves using hoops and straps, all the time warning her that a misjudgement or mistiming could be fatal.

Later, Maggie sat by the fire outside the caravan, and gazed up at the bright canopy of stars wishing Josh was with her. The stars were never visible from the Home and she imagined Josh's mouth dropping in awe at the glittering constellations, and then his grin, and his voice saying, "It's nice here, Mags. Let's stay."

She poked at the flames with a stick, filled with guilt. She had not gone back to find him. "Don't cry," a deep voice said high above her. Looking up she saw the same huge creature she had seen in the parade rising above her, bigger than the caravan. He glowed in a bright pink and purple jumper. His eyes were kind, but his tusks were pin sharp. His trunk reached out and tickled her ears. "Hello, I'm, I'm… Oh dear, who am I?" he said, rubbing his forehead with his snake-like arm. Madam Lulu stepped out of the caravan.

"You're McTavish, the elephant."

McTavish pulled something from his back and draped a knitted blue cardigan over Maggie's shoulders.

"It's a Welcome-to-the-Circus present."

Maggie struggled into his gift. It reached down to her

feet, and the sleeves scraped the floor. The buttonholes were big enough for plates.

"It's lovely."

"I knitted it myself," said McTavish proudly.

Madam Lulu gave him a disapproving stare and disappeared back into the caravan.

"You look like Aisha," McTavish said.

Maggie inched forwards. "Aisha?"

McTavish lowered his voice. "Aisha went missing after Fozia. Alice went missing after Aisha and Loka went missing after Alice. There are plenty other people who've gone missing and not just from this circus. I've heard from my elephant network in Africa and India that it's a worldwide problem. Be careful, you might be next."

Madam Lulu yelled from inside the caravan. "Go away, we're busy!"

The elephant trumpeted loudly and lumbered off muttering to himself.

Madam Lulu leaned out of the window. "You're not wearing that cardigan in the ring. It's too heavy. You won't be able to move."

Maggie pulled the cardigan around her, overwhelmed by the change in her life.

4

Josh scrubbed at the dishes with a tight knot in his throat. It had been weeks since Maggie had left. Where was she? Miss Scribbens prowled the Home's stone floors, wailing wildly.

"Gone! Escaped. Ungrateful, wicked child, deserting her own Miss Scribbens who is but a saint, full of love and kindness," she cried, turning on Josh and shaking him. "Thick as thieves you two. You must know where she is."

"I don't, I promise I don't," Josh said through chattering teeth.

She sent Carry-On and the children into the city to look for Maggie. Hours later, they returned without her. Josh heard the slap of Miss Scribbens' feet heading towards the scullery and hid behind the door. She slammed it open, flattening him against the wall. Her fingers hooked into his shoulders. "That little rat must have taught you a trick or two. Get out there and bring me back the same rich pickings."

"No!" Josh cried. "I'm no good. Not like Maggie. Send someone else."

"The others are useless. That girl is the queen of pocket delving. She knows what's worth having. Eh, darling boy?"

She handed him an empty bag and forced him through the gates. He scoured the dark streets looking for pickable pockets, but his hands were too cold and his legs too weak. He returned empty handed.

"Good for nothing! Get back to washing dishes," Miss Scribbens screamed, and locked him in the scullery.

Josh warmed his hands on the copper boiler, unable to quell his rising anger. Maggie had broken her promise. She had said she would never leave without him but she had, and there was still no word from her.

A loud crash echoed throughout the kitchen. His heart skipped. Maggie? A key turned in the scullery door.

"Watcha mate," a cheeky voice said.

Josh stared in amazement as a small monkey leapt onto the table scattering pots and pans. He wore a red velvet waistcoat, a green cravat and red pantaloons over grey fur. He raised a bowler hat from his head in greeting.

"Better sit down, mate. You look a bit shaky on yer ham 'n' eggs."

"Ham 'n' eggs?"

"Legs, matey."

"What are you doing here?"

"Agent Jackson. That's me. AJ to me mates. Just visitin'."

"Agent? That's a funny name."

"Crikey, not very bright are we? You humans are all the same. Don't use your loaf."

AJ touched his head with a silver-topped cane and skipped across the table.

"An agent is a detective. A spy. A sleuth. I'm on a mission. Top secret like. So secret, I can't even tell myself."

Josh glanced nervously around him.

"You'd better go, AJ. Miss Scribbens and Carry-On will be back soon. They'll kill you if they find you here."

"Awright little geeza. Keep yer Barnet Fair on. Gentleman Agent Jackson ain't afraid of nothin'."

Josh heard the iron gates open and ran to the window.

"It's them. Quick, hide," he said, and lifted a resisting AJ from the table. There was a struggle as he pushed the monkey into a cupboard.

"Get your mitts off me. I ain't scarperin' from no-one," AJ hissed, baring sharp, tiny teeth as Josh slammed the door in his face.

Miss Scribbens burst into the room dragging a sack. Carry-On hopped behind her. Muffled cries filled the room as she cut the string around the sack's neck. A frightened brown face poked out.

"Come on out, ragamuffin. Thought you could outrun us did you. This'll teach you."

She shook the sack. A small boy tumbled to the floor.

"Ragamuffin, ragamuffin," the crow mimicked, pecking at his feet.

"Careful, Carry-On. This little petal could be the making of us. He has fingers as fevery as that vermin child – the one who has deserted her loved ones like drowning innocents on a dark, cold sea."

Miss Scribbens raised her hands to her brow and made as if to faint. The boy burst into tears and begged, "Take me back to the arches. Anything is better than being here with you lot."

She squeezed his face until he squirmed. "Ungrateful wretch. You thought you had my purse didn't you, but I caught you. Good try. We are very impressed, aren't we Carry-On? From now on you will be nice to your Miss

34

Scribbens – as if she were your own dear mother – if you ever had one."

Carry-On cawed wildly and flapped his wings.

"Let's see if you're as good as you were when you so deftly picked my purse," Miss Scribbens said. "We shall do well by you if I am inclined right. But first, a little test. Now, watch. I shall busy myself like a lady occupied and you shall pick my pocket."

Josh looked on in horror as Miss Scribbens busied herself opening and shutting drawers. The boy followed, shaking and whimpering.

She reached the cupboard and opened it. AJ flew at her with a shattering scream. Miss Scribbens tottered backwards. AJ seized her neck. Carry-On swooped down and AJ slashed at its wings with his tail.

"Quick," said Josh, grabbing the boy.

They darted through the scullery and into the yard. Josh helped him over the gates. AJ was already gone.

"Run," Josh said. "Run as fast as you can."

The boy flashed a grateful smile.

"Look out for my friend Maggie," Josh said. "Looks like me. Short hair. Tell her I…"

The boy leapt onto a passing cart and disappeared around the corner. Feeling more alone than ever, Josh returned to the kitchen. Miss Scribbens lay upon the floor, weighed down by her pockets and jewellery.

"Carry-On, go after that monkey. He has my hat."

The bird limped out of the door, leaving a trail of black feathers behind him.

Miss Scribbens struggled to sit up. "That creature was a mate of yours, wasn't he?" she said

"No. I only ever saw a monkey with a hurdy-gurdy."

"Someone let you out of the scullery, eh? Who?"

"You forgot to lock it."

"Liar. You helped our new little Fever Fingers escape, didn't you?"

"I tried to stop him."

"They'll be dead meat if I get my hands on them."

Josh sank to the floor. How could Maggie have left him alone like this?

5

Josh's hands scrabbled around the dark attic searching for the rags that were his bed. Something crackled. A sheet of folded paper fell from one of his pockets. Moving to where moonlight fell through broken slates, Josh unfolded the paper and stared at the muddled handwriting. Slowly and with difficulty he read:

My dear Josh, This letter is from me, Maggie, and is written by a friend, my hand being slow. It has been secretly delivered.

I miss you very much, Josh. Sometimes I cry myself to sleep thinking of you. I didn't mean to leave you. I was taken, not on purpose, but it has worked out right. I could have come back, but I could not stop myself eating the apple pie and gammon. I am all washed and eat every day and my bed is soft. The lady here is very kind to me. Not like Miss Scribbens. She says you will be with me soon.

We are travelling far away all the time. But it is nice here. The lady says I will soon fly like a bird.

I miss you very much. My friend says, DO NOT GIVE UP HOPE.

Lots of hugs to MY BEST MATE,

Mags

PS When you have read this, PLEASE TEAR IT UP.

Josh read the letter over and over again. What did she mean, "fly like a bird", and who had delivered it? It must have been AJ. Or, was Miss Scribbens playing tricks on him? He heard the stairs creak under the weight of her steps and quickly hid the letter in a crack in a rafter. He lay down upon the floor and pretended to be asleep. Her shadow fell across him, hovered and returned to the stairs.

He was woken in the morning by Miss Scribbens shouting up at him. "Come down now you little brat! I need mutton chops for breakfast. Make sure they are well bloodied. Hurry!"

She kicked Josh into the street. He ran to the butchers, the wind racing with him as he pushed through heavy rain.

"Oi, Scribbens boy!" someone shouted.

Josh ignored the call. A small stone bounced off his

head. He turned around and recognised the boy from the sack.

"I've found out something about your Maggie," the boy said, smiling against the rain slashing his face.

Josh pulled him into a side alley. Rats splashed through puddles and ran over their feet. "Where is she?"

"It might be her. It might not."

Josh held him fast.

"Tell me."

The boy told him he had heard about a girl resembling Maggie being chased by a man and a policeman.

"They lost her in a crowd watching a circus parade."

"What else?"

"My friend said she was taken into a caravan. He never saw her leave."

"Where's the circus now?"

The boy shrugged his shoulders. "No way of knowing. Circuses travel all over. This one's supposed to be good. It's got man-eating tigers, an elephant and a lady who can fold herself into an envelope."

"What's it called?"

"Mrs Gumbo's something Circus."

Josh looked downcast. "I'll never find her. They're probably miles away by now."

"Circuses always come back," the boy said. "They go around in circles, one place to another. She probably likes it. Anything's better than that horrible place you're living in."

Feathers rustled in the darkness. Josh looked across at the dark shadow settling on a pile of stinking rubbish. Carry-On's eyes fixed sharply upon them. The boy gave Josh a friendly slap on the shoulder and sped off, disappearing into the street. Josh followed, splashing noisily through puddles. The crow's wings sliced through the air after him.

"I see you. I see you," it squawked and dived down to stab at Josh's face and neck with its beak. Still running, Josh lashed out at the bird. He didn't stop until he heard the loud smack of Carry-On hitting a street gas light. It slid down the post and landed on its back, its feathered legs rigid in the air. Josh burst into laughter and continued running.

6

"It's a big day – your first rehearsal in the Big Top," Madam Lulu said, holding up a sequined one-piece suit with tiny silver wings attached to the back. Maggie took it reluctantly and slowly dressed.

"I don't want to do it. I'm not ready," she said.

"I shall say if you're ready or not, and in my expert opinion, you are," Madam Lulu said, flexing her fingers and stretching her arms.

Maggie stood at the caravan door, sparkling like a silver fairy. She stared across at the Big Top.

It rose high above the caravans, its canvas lurching to one side on its poles. Hammers rang in the air as the circus crew drove pegs into the ground and secured the tent with ropes. Madam Lulu pushed her down the steps and led her into the Big Top. Maggie gasped. It was like the cathedral

41

she had once hidden in while running from the police, except instead of an altar, the tent had a performance ring in its centre surrounded by rough wooden benches. She breathed in the smell of sawdust and looked up at the rigging. It was several times higher than the training equipment and looked as far away as the moon. Madam Lulu pushed her forwards and McTavish and the tigers cheered.

"Watch me!" Madam Lulu shouted, climbing the rope like a monkey towards the platform. Maggie watched as she spun from one trapeze to another, barely touching the bars, her body twisting like a fish. She zoomed close to their heads and dive bombed to the floor, scattering sawdust into the air. Everyone held their breath in horror waiting for her body to hit the floor but she suddenly flipped and propelled herself upwards. She stretched her arms and swooped like a vast bird towards a trapeze. Within seconds she was swinging upside down from the bar, pulling funny faces at everyone. She flipped herself back onto the platform.

"Watch me do The Cannonball," she yelled, curling herself into a ball, and ricocheting from one side of the Big Top to another.

Maggie clenched her fists apprehensively. She could never imagine herself hurtling through the air with such a mighty whoosh. Would Madam Lulu send her back to the Home if she failed her?

"One day soon, you'll fly like a bird," Madam Lulu shouted at her, landing back on the platform. "You're better than all the other girls."

"The missing girls?" Maggie shouted back.

Madam Lulu curled her legs round the rope and hung upside down, smiling.

Maggie felt a tap on her arm. Dewi stood beside her with a small monkey on her back. He twirled a cane and wore a green striped suit and a red silk cravat. He raised his top hat and flashed a smile.

"Agent Jackson at your service. AJ to my mates," he said, tapping his nose with his cane. "Anything of a peculiar nature is my business."

"You must have a lot of business. Everything here is peculiar," Maggie said.

The monkey cocked his head. "You look like you could be a mate of mine, so call me AJ."

He held out a hand and she shook it. It felt like a small mouse.

"Your turn," Madam Lulu shouted.

Maggie looked desperately around her for an excuse to delay the inevitable. McTavish complacently knitted a tea

43

cosy while the three tigers lounged on circus seats, lazily filing their claws. A clown wandered in and sat beside them. He looked sadly up at the roof of the Big Top.

"You won't be able to go up there," he said. "You'll fall if you do. My friend did. She's had to stay in bed ever since." Huge tears splashed down his face.

"Shut up Gloomy. You and your Grizzling Brothers are such miseries," Rara said.

Gloomy cried even more. "I'm only doing my job. Yesterday I got lost and couldn't find myself, today my mother was robbed, and yesterday my father fell from a ladder and the milk has turned sour for miles around."

"I thought clowns were supposed to make people laugh," Maggie said, staring nervously at the rope swinging from the platform.

"The Grizzling Brothers are the world's best clowns. People travel miles to see us and have a good cry. They always feel better after."

"Will you go away if I promise to tell you a very sad story later?" Maggie said. "You're putting me off."

Gloomy shuffled out of the Big Top, tears bouncing from the floor as he walked. Maggie breathed deeply, pressed her palms together as if in prayer and approached the rope. Her hands were white with chalk powder to prevent her

44

from slipping. Even after all the training and rehearsals, she knew deep down she was about to disappoint everyone. She stared up at the rope and turned away as if to leave the ring. I'm only good at pickpocketing, she told herself.

"You can't put it off any longer, sweetie," Rara said. "We'll catch you if you fall. But you won't. We've seen you train. You're exceptional."

The tiger spun her around with her paws so that Maggie faced the rope. There was no escape. Taking a deep breath, she placed one hand after the other and hauled herself up the rope before twining her legs around it and scampering up. The higher she climbed, the fainter her audience's cheers became. She dared not look down. Madam Lulu reached out and pulled her up onto the platform. She looked down and wobbled, suddenly dizzy. Madam Lulu held her steady.

"If you fall, remember I am your safety net," she said. "You have done well to get this far, my beauty. None of my apprentices achieved so much so quickly. You are the best."

The encouragement gave Maggie the courage to look around her. Light filtered through the canvas above her and several trapezes, rungs and hoops hung at different lengths from the rigging. A tightrope stretched high across the tent. The training had improved her balance, but flying to and from a trapeze so high above the ground involved great strength and perfect timing.

Madam Lulu pointed to a trapeze an arm's length away and instructed her to swing from it towards the tent's roof before returning to the platform.

"Try not to make your movements jerky so the trapeze doesn't jolt. It's like music – you have to stay with the rhythm," she said and pulled the trapeze to the platform.

Maggie gripped her hands tightly around the bar, and with a slight push of her legs swung away from the platform.

"Don't look down," she whispered to herself as she led the momentum of the trapeze.

"Swing higher!" Madam Lulu shouted.

Maggie used her legs to swing higher.

"Stop pointing your feet so much, or your toes will curl."

The air rushed past her like a wind of her own making.

"Come back to the platform," Madam Lulu instructed.

Maggie's back was to the platform. How could she land on it when she couldn't see it? She'd done it before, but suddenly her mind was blank. She looked down at the small figures staring up at her and forced a nervous smile.

"When I tell you, swing your legs back, put your feet on the platform and stop," said Madam Lulu.

McTavish covered his eyes with his trunk. "I can't bear to look."

"Don't be such a pussycat," Dewi said. "If she falls, we'll catch her."

"You'll be one squashed tiger," McTavish said as Maggie swung above them like a silver star and landed neatly back on the platform.

"Bravo!" the animals cheered.

Encouraged by their applause, Maggie swung away from the platform before Madam Lulu could stop her.

"No, no!" she screamed. "You're not gripping correctly. Come back."

A loud groan rose in the air as Maggie threw herself forward so forcefully she lost control of the trapeze. It jolted her backwards and forwards as if to shake her off. The weight of her body slowed it down until finally she hung suspended above the ring. She kicked her legs in panic.

"Don't kick, bring your legs together and pull your body back," Madam Lulu shouted.

"I can't, I can't," Maggie screamed as her fingers weakened around the bar.

"I'm coming to get you," Madam Lulu said, and grabbed at a trapeze above the platform. Somersaulting over the bar so that she hung by the back of her knees, she swung backwards and forwards towards Maggie gaining enough momentum to reach Maggie's ankles.

"Let go NOW!" she commanded as her fingers touched Maggie's ankles. In that instant Maggie's fingers slipped from the bar.

"Aaaaaaaagh!" she screamed, clawing at the air and hurtling towards the circus ring.

The animals watched in horror as Maggie sped towards them. McTavish thundered into the ring and held out his trunk to catch her. The tigers collided with him in their rush to catch their falling friend. They lay in a helpless tangle as Maggie continued to speed towards them.

The floor was inches from her nose. This is the end, she thought. A blast of warm air suddenly ballooned around her and she hovered momentarily above the ring. Madam Lulu's arms curled around her.

"Hold on, little star" she said, and, holding Maggie tightly, flew with her to the top of the tent.

"I'll never be able to fly," Maggie said, bursting into tears when they landed on the platform.

Madam Lulu crossed her arms, "Of course you will, dearie. We all make mistakes…"

"Yes but, I… I..."

"… and when we do we must learn from them. You did not listen to me."

Maggie sniffed.

"Your debut performance will be in the next town we stop at."

"When will that be?"

Madam Lulu laughed and her eyes lit up. "Who knows?" she said. "You will be ready, but we have a lot to do. Today you dropped like a stone, but tomorrow you'll fly like a bird – just like the wonderful, miracle-performing Madam Lulu!"

She stretched out her arms, gave a loud whoop, jumped off the platform and swooped upwards with such force Maggie thought she might burst through the Big Top.

7

Miss Scribbens picked at a boil on her chin. "I smell dastardly doings," she said.

Her heavily hooded eyes searched through the Home. Children huddled in corners, bats shivered and closed their wings. She sent Carry-On to the attic.

"I don't care if you've hurt a wing. Search everywhere. Don't come down till you've found something."

From behind the scullery door, Josh listened to Miss Scribbens muttering to herself. "That boy's a good-for-nothing. He couldn't pick a baby's pocket, let alone a gentleman's. He can't wash up either. The dishes come out of the sink as dirty as they went in. He's a liability. It is only kindful, pitying Miss Scribbens that keeps him here."

If they found the letter, he was in trouble. He should

have followed Maggie's instructions and torn it up, but it was the only thing he had left of her.

He looked around at the scullery's dark, dingy walls, the filthy greasy water in the lead sink, the Home's cracked bowls, rusting cutlery and Miss Scribbens' beautiful china. Now that Maggie was gone, the Home was even more unbearable.

He heard Carry-On hopping up the stairs. It was some time before he heard it hop back down again. An eerie silence was broken by the unfolding of paper and a loud shriek. "A letter. We are after her now, Carry-On."

Miss Scribbens read the letter and grunted, "Travelling and flying? What does she think she is – a pigeon?"

Carry-On's beak scissored open in a raucous laugh. "Circus, circus, circus," he said, sounding exactly like Miss Scribbens.

Josh heard her bash Carry-On with what sounded like a saucepan. "Circus? Why didn't you tell me this before, numbskull?" she screamed. "I've been humiliated by the one to whom I gave fortune and shelter. How dare she? I had hoped she was bleeding in a gutter somewhere!"

Carry-On stroked her neck with his beak. She brushed him away.

"Instead, she's in a circus with a bunch of performing

good-for-nothings who are no doubt profiting from her nifty fingers, instead of me, her one and only Miss Scribbens."

Josh looked frantically around him. The window was too small for him to squeeze through. The doors into the kitchen and yard were locked. A flurry of footsteps headed towards the scullery. He scooped the washing-up water into a pail and stood trembling before the door. It smashed open. Miss Scribbens stood before him waving the letter. Josh flung the water at her and ran into the kitchen. He aimed a plate at Carry-On before running out. Cheering children filled the corridor and pushed him forwards towards the main door while forming a barrier against Miss Scribbens and her crow. Josh crossed the yard, scaled the high gates, gave an exultant wave and ran into the street.

8

Maggie sat on the steps of Madam Lulu's caravan. A bright moon shone directly on the Big Top and a gentle wind tugged at its ropes. Fiddles played and the tigers beat drums and laughed and sang in chorus. McTavish trumpeted as a circle of flames spun outside the fire-eater's tent and acrobats tumbled over each other on the grass. She wanted to join them, but her body was tired and ached after her first rehearsal in the Big Top. If only Josh and the children at the Scribbens Home could be sat around the camp fire with her. They would be singing and laughing till dawn. She gazed up at the moon, feeling suddenly alone. Something stirred behind her.

"Psst," a voice hissed.

Maggie jumped up and looked beneath the caravan.

Two sharp, bright eyes stared back at her. She drew back and AJ leapt up towards her, a finger held over his mouth.

"Don't say anything," he said. "Just follow me."

Maggie hesitated.

"Don't worry. I won't hurt you."

"Where are we going?"

"To Brimstone's."

"Who's Brimstone?"

"He's the circus magician. Performs magic; makes things appear and disappear, turns things into things they're not. He's not been here long. Mrs Gumbo fired the last one, but she liked Brimstone. She's gone missing, too."

"I haven't seen him."

"No-one ever does, except when he performs. He doesn't go out much."

The monkey smiled and pointed his cane to a purple and red caravan with drawn curtains and thick black smoke curling from its chimney. She hadn't noticed it before.

Maggie shivered. "Why are we going there? It looks a bit scary."

"Because I'm a detective and I'm lookin' for Clues."

"What are Clues?"

"You humans don't know nuffin', do you? Clues are sign posts. They point you in the right direction."

Maggie looked puzzled.

"Clues will lead us to whoever, or whatever, is causing the disappearances."

"You think Brimstone is responsible?"

AJ tapped his nose with his cane. "Let's say, I'm explorin' all avenues and he's a Suspect."

He led her towards Brimstone's caravan and crept up the rickety wooden steps to put an ear to the door.

He shook his head and mouthed, "He's out."

He pulled at the door with his tiny hands until it rattled. Maggie looked nervously around her. "We need the key," she said.

AJ leapt over the steps and looked up at her, laughing.

"How are we going to get his key?"

A shadow passed over them, blotting out the moon. A tall, stringy man with oily black hair and chalk-white skin stared down at them. His eyes pierced them like long, cold needles and held them as if in an arm lock.

"Quick, scarper," AJ said, struggling to lift a leg from the ground. Brimstone walked slowly around them, prodding them gently with his cane.

"Pleased to meet you, sir," Maggie said.

Brimstone's smile lifted his thick handlebar moustache and he raised his top hat. A dove flew out.

"Introduce me, Jackson," he said.

"This is Miss Maggie."

"Ah yes, the new girl."

He offered Maggie a thin, gloved hand.

"Who are you, sir?" Maggie asked, flinching at the heat of his palm.

"I am Brimstone, the world's Most Magical Magician. You might say I am the STAR of the circus – wouldn't you, Jackson?"

"You would, sir," AJ said, curling his tail behind him and sniggering.

Brimstone wiggled his fingers in the air, plunged them into a pocket and pulled out a short black stick, with silver ends. He caressed it with his hands and waved it delicately in the air.

"This, my friends, is the most powerful wand you will ever encounter. Its tricks are astounding. In the proper hands – like mine – it will do anything you want it to, otherwise it's no more than a twig."

AJ stared at the wand. "You haven't done very well with it so far," he said. "That rabbit you disappeared in a top hat the other day hasn't come back yet, and the fire-eater says the silver belt you vanished and brought back as a snake has never seen since. Why don't you give the wand to me? I'd know how to use it."

Brimstone glared and pointed the wand at him.

"No way, and careful what you say, Jackson. Wands don't like insults."

"It's you I'm insulting, not the wand," AJ said. "A wand is only as good as its master. What magic school did you go to?"

"Mingles Magic School for the Retired. It wasn't the best. It's had dreadful reviews. But once I left, I was able to expand my magical skills. I am, you could say, self-tutored and am now one of the best." He stroked his moustache and with a flourish pointed the wand at AJ.

"Where did you get that wand from? I bet you stole it."

"I am not a thief," Brimstone said. "The wand found me. It just dropped from nowhere and landed at my feet."

AJ stepped towards Brimstone as if to snatch the wand from him, but his hat suddenly lifted from his head and appeared in the magician's hands. AJ rushed forward to retrieve it, but Brimstone placed it on the wand and twirled it so fast it spun into the air.

"Hey!" AJ shouted.

Brimstone smiled. "Don't worry. You shall have your hat back, monkey."

The hat hovered high above them. Brimstone pointed the wand at it, but the hat remained fixed. He rubbed the wand on his sleeve and checked it for specks of dirt. He pointed it again at the hat, but it only moved further away from them until it was a mere speck in the sky. Brimstone shook the wand, and the almost invisible hat turned into a small, moonlit cloud.

Maggie stared open-mouthed as heavy raindrops fell from the cloud and drenched them.

"I'll get you for this, Brimstone," AJ shrieked, leaping out of the rain.

Brimstone appeared shocked and dried the wand with a handkerchief. He blew on it, spat on it, shook it, kissed it and did everything he could to get it to work. But the rain continued to pour down.

"Please do something," Maggie said, wet and shivering.

"Hey presto!" Brimstone shouted, pointing the wand at the cloud. It still rained.

"Give me my hat back," AJ shouted at the cloud.

Brimstone held the wand close to his mouth and whispered to it. He drew ever-increasing circles in the air before pointing it at the cloud.

They all watched as the cloud evaporated and AJ's hat fell to the floor, soaked and battered.

"I told you I'd get it back didn't I?" Brimstone said, looking surprised. "Wasn't that cloud spectacular? What a piece of magic, eh?"

He returned the wand to his pocket and bowed graciously to Maggie. His breath burnt her skin.

They watched him saunter away. AJ looked forlornly at his dripping hat. "I don't trust him. His magic is weird and ever since he's arrived, four girls have disappeared, as well as Mrs Gumbo, Tearful – one of the Grizzling Brothers – lots of rabbits, doves, pigeons and kittens. Audience valuables have mysteriously disappeared. One woman fired a pistol at him after he turned her gold watch into a teapot and couldn't magic it back."

"Perhaps his wand isn't working," Maggie said, shivering in her wet clothes.

"A poor workman blames his tools," AJ said. "It's him. I'm certain of it."

"What shall we do?"

"Being a detective, I need to investigate, startin' with a search of his caravan, but I don't know how we can get in without him knowin'."

Maggie swung a small brass key under AJ's nose.

"Blimey," he said. "What's that?"

Maggie nodded her head and smiled. "It's the key to Brimstone's caravan."

9

Josh curled up inside a shop doorway, cold, hungry and alone. He had run as fast as he could and as far away as he could, but was still not out of the city. The turrets of the Scribbens' Home still rose behind him, and even worse, he did not know where he was going. All he knew was that he was looking for a circus and that Maggie was travelling with it. Daylight faded and the crowds thinned out. He smelt roasting chestnuts and watched a cart pass by laden with boxes of apples. He put his hands into his empty pockets and sighed. He closed his eyes and tried to sleep but felt colder and hungrier. There was only one thing he could do. He tried to stand but swayed dizzily from side to side. Holding onto the doorway, he stepped into the street and watched as people passed him by. He spotted a well-dressed elderly gentleman with a silver moustache carrying a small leather bag. Mustering what little strength he had, Josh ran up to him and pulled at the bag. The man grabbed him but Josh slipped away and tried to run. He looked behind him: the man was running after him, his belly wobbling. A pain shot across Josh's chest and he could not breathe. He doubled over and crumpled to the floor. His pursuer stood over him.

"I'm sorry sir," Josh gasped, "but I'm starving. I just want some coins to buy me a pie."

The man lifted him up and peered into Josh's pale and frightened face. He had kind brown eyes and a slight, compassionate smile. "You don't look very well. You need a good meal," he said. "I'm taking you home with me." He picked up his bag and, holding Josh's arm, walked him to the kerb and called for a carriage.

Josh had no idea where he was going and didn't care. The horse's hooves drummed in his head and the man remained silent, occasionally stroking his moustache. After a while he tapped on the carriage window, and it drew to a halt. He helped Josh out onto the pavement and drew some keys from his pocket. Josh stared up at the grand terraced house. It had pillars at the door and a big brass knocker.

"Is this house yours, sir?"

The man smiled. "Yes, I'm afraid it is. It is the home of Mr Horatio Banerjee."

"Is that you?" Josh said timidly.

"I'm afraid so."

"Why are you afraid to be who you are?" Josh asked and Mr Banerjee burst into loud booming laughter.

"A very good question, young man, and one that must be answered."

Josh shook his head, perplexed, briefly forgetting his fatigue and hunger.

"Welcome," Mr Banerjee said, throwing open the door and leading him across a marble hall. He flung open another door and ushered Josh into a room crammed with ornately carved furniture, gilt framed paintings and glass cabinets full of strange, labelled objects. A fire roared in a huge, ornate fireplace. Josh smelt burning wood and cinnamon.

"Sit down, young sir," Mr Banerjee said, pointing to an old, faded couch. Josh sank into its cushions, grateful for its velvet softness and for the fire's warmth.

"I'm going to ask cook to rustle something up," Mr Banerjee said and disappeared.

Josh closed his eyes and sank into a deep sleep. When he woke, the room was lit by lamps and the curtains were drawn. Mr Banerjee was nowhere to be seen. Someone tapped on the door and a short, neat woman entered carrying a large tray. She set it on a table and beckoned him over.

"You should be eating in the kitchen, but the master says you are too weak. Here's your knife and fork, and a napkin. Mind your manners when you're eating. I don't want any mess."

Josh gazed at the steaming plate of mutton stew, dumplings, potatoes and peas.

"Is this all mine?" he asked incredulously.

The woman's severe face relaxed into a smile.

"It is, and you have Mr Banerjee to thank for it – and me – who's known hereabouts as Mrs Grubb. Best cook in town."

"Thank you Mrs Grubb," Josh said, shovelling a fork piled with potato into his mouth. Within minutes the plate was empty. He looked up at her, still hungry but afraid to ask for more. She nodded her head, took the tray and returned with another full plate. He felt he could eat forever. At the end of the fourth serving, he slumped back and burped.

"I've never seen anyone eat so much. Watch you don't burst. Your innards will be all over the room and I don't like messes to clear up," Mrs Grubb said and, laughing, took up the tray and left the room.

All around him clocks struck different hours, noisy and shrill. He peeped out from the room. Mr Banerjee was nowhere to be seen. He didn't know whether to stay or leave. He wandered into the hall and, gazing at the front door, thought of the cold streets outside, the damp doorways, the rats, stray dogs and Miss Scribbens. He turned back into the room, lay on the couch and fell into a deep sleep. He awoke in a warm soft bed. A fire crackled in the fireplace and his clothes were draped over a chair like old rags. He looked down at his crisp white nightshirt in disbelief. Mrs Grubb peered around the door.

"The master says to give you these," she said and laid out trousers, a shirt, a waistcoat and jacket on the bed. "He says to wash and get dressed as soon as you can and to go to his study. I will bring you hot water."

"Are you real?" Josh asked.

"Of course I am, as real as you are. You can pinch me if you like," Mrs Grubb said, laughing.

Josh leant back against the pillows.

"I feel like I'm dreaming," he said and thought of Carry-On poking him awake with its sharp beak.

"Make the most of it. Dreams don't last long," Mrs Grubb said, and left the room.

Josh did not feel like himself in his new clothes. Maggie would not recognise him if she saw him. His heart sank. Where was she?

A maid escorted him to the study. He knocked on the door.

"Come in," Mr Banerjee said. Josh stepped into the room and stared around him. Its walls were lined with books, skulls, bones, stuffed birds and animals. Strange creatures stared out at him from jars of liquid and a stuffed wolf behind the door looked real enough to make him jump.

"Nothing you see here is alive. It's like a graveyard," Mr Banerjee said. He was sitting behind a huge ebony bureau full of drawers and covered in papers. Plucking a quill from behind his ear and waving it in the air, he beckoned Josh to sit. "Now, young man, I forgot to ask you your name."

"It's Josh, sir."

"And your second name?"

"I don't know, sir. I've never had one."

"You're an orphan?"

Josh nodded. "You don't need to tell me your story," Mr

Banerjee said. "I can guess. You were in some awful home and ran away."

Josh stared wide eyed at him. How did he know?

Mr Banerjee perched a pair of glasses at the end of his nose and peered at him. "I suppose this home taught pickpocketing and little else."

"Yes," Josh said miserably." But me and Mags, we taught ourselves to read – a bit."

"There are plenty of children like you, Josh, lost in the streets. It's nothing to be ashamed of."

Tears pricked Josh's eyes. "I'm sorry," he said. "I didn't mean to steal from you. I just needed money to find the circus."

"The circus?"

"I'm looking for my friend, Maggie. She ran away from the Home too, but without me."

Mr Banerjee looked thoughtful for a long time. "This Maggie," he said, "does she look like you, a fast runner, and a very good pickpocket?"

Josh sat bolt upright. "Yes, yes! Have you seen her? I've been looking for her everywhere. She's my best friend."

Mr Banerjee leant back in his chair and dipped the quill in and out of a pot of ink.

"She stole something from me. I want it back. I chased

her but she disappeared into a crowd. When the circus passed by, she disappeared."

"Do you know the name of the circus, sir?"

"Yes – Mrs Gumbo's Flying Circus."

Josh leapt from his chair. "That's it! The boy said it was Mrs Gumbo's something Circus. I have to find her."

"So do I," Mr Banerjee said. "We shall look for her together."

10

Maggie watched Brimstone's caravan and reported daily to AJ on what she had seen – except she never saw anything. The magician had not left his caravan for two days.

"What does he do in there? He doesn't even go out to the shops," Maggie said. AJ shrugged his shoulders.

"Practises his magic, I suppose. He needs to."

They looked across at the caravan that stood apart from the others. Smoke no longer belched from its chimney.

"He can't stay in there forever. He's got to leave at some point." Maggie said, and jumped as the caravan door flew open with a bang and Brimstone stepped out. He looked around him and turned to lock the door.

"He must have a spare key," Maggie said.

"I hope he hasn't changed the lock."

"Only one way to find out," Maggie said, watching Brimstone disappear between tents and wagons. Making sure they weren't being watched, Maggie and AJ crept towards the caravan. Maggie turned the key and the door opened. They stepped into the darkness. AJ pulled a candle from his pocket and lit it. They stared around in astonishment.

The inside of the caravan was much larger than it appeared from the outside. Its walls were black and shone like patent leather shoes. It smelt of damp crowds, stale food and rabbit and pigeon poo. It was empty except for brightly coloured boxes of different sizes scattered around the caravan.

Maggie locked the door and AJ peered through a magnifying glass into one of the boxes.

"What are you looking for?"

"Clues," he said and held up several thin white hairs. He held them up to the magnifying glass. "Nuns and habits."

"What?"

"Rabbits."

Maggie picked up two white feathers from the floor.

"Richard the Third – bird," AJ said.

"Are they Clues?"

"No. Every magician uses doves, snakes, white rabbits. Some even use horses and crocodiles in their shows."

Maggie checked the boxes – they were all empty. She stared around the strange caravan. There was nowhere to cook, sleep, sit or eat. Just boxes. The candlelight cast giant shadows around the walls. "Let's get out of here," she said with a shiver.

They started for the door but stopped when they heard someone outside.

"Quick," Maggie whispered and jumped into the nearest and largest box. AJ blew out the candle and leapt in to join her. They closed the lid and huddled in the dark as a key turned in the lock and footsteps crossed the caravan. Maggie lifted the lid a little way and peeped out. "He must have another key, or he has used the wand," she whispered.

Brimstone stood in the centre of the caravan with two brightly coloured parrots on his arm. He picked up a small bright red box and pushed one of the parrots into it. It squawked, flapped its wings and pecked at Brimstone, while its friend flew frantically around the caravan desperate for an exit. Brimstone pushed the parrot into the box and slammed the lid down. He took the wand from his pocket, tapped the box three times and waited. Maggie watched as he opened the box, peered inside, turned it upside down and shook it. An orange feather drifted to the floor. Maggie's eyes widened. Where was the parrot? Brimstone closed the lid again and gave the box another hard whack.

"Watch how Brimstone, Master Magician, will make the parrot reappear," he announced to an imaginary audience. He opened the lid again. No parrot.

"Where are you, stupid bird?" he said, waving his wand in the air, before giving up. He dropped the box to the floor with a sigh and buried his head in his hands. "The monkey's right, I am no good," he said, taking an egg from his pocket. He held it up between his thumb and forefinger. "This egg will disappear before your very eyes, and its place will be taken by the one and only corpse-eating Indian vulture," he said, blowing on it. The egg exploded with a loud crack. Yoke and egg white dripped down his hand. He waited, but despite some frantic waving of the wand, nothing happened. "Another failure," he groaned. "I can't even magic an omelette."

Maggie lowered the lid, feeling sorry for the magician. The box grew warmer. AJ's fur brushed damp and warm against her. His breathing grew shallow. He wouldn't survive if they had to stay in the box for much longer. She heard Brimstone muttering angrily to himself and pacing up and down the caravan. His footsteps turned and headed towards them. Maggie grabbed AJ's hand as Brimstone sat on the box with a heavy bump and drummed his fingers against the side for what seemed a long time. AJ and Maggie struggled for breath as if the air had turned solid. Suddenly there was a loud banging on the door. Brimstone jumped up. "Who is it? I don't like visitors," he said.

"McTavish, sir," the elephant boomed.

Brimstone threw open the door.

"Yes?"

"There's a problem in the Big Top. Madam Lulu is stuck in mid-air, and we thought, you being the Tallest and Best Magician in the World, you would be able to unstick her."

Brimstone puffed out his chest. "You have come to the right person, McTavish. Let's go."

The door slammed. Maggie and AJ leapt from the box, gulping air. Strangely, a fire blazed, and a long, thin bed, a chair and a table stood nearby. White mice ran around the floor.

"There was nothing here when we came in," said Maggie rubbing her eyes.

"Never mind that, lets scarper." AJ pulled her towards the door.

Maggie rushed into the Big Top. Madam Lulu greeted her from Brimstone's shoulders.

"Don't worry, dearest angel. This brave man rescued me. I was seized by a cramp on the rope and couldn't move," she said, winking at Maggie. Brimstone bent down and she leapt off him like a mountain goat.

Brimstone straightened his jacket, smoothed his moustache and, bowing to Madam Lulu, walked out of the Big Top, the roar of congratulatory cheers ringing in his ears.

"What was all that about?" AJ asked as soon as he was out of earshot.

Rara approached them, tail curled and eyes narrowed to slits. "We saw you go into Brimstone's caravan," she said.

"We were worried," Dewi added.

"We thought he might magic you away," said Citra.

"When we saw him go in and you didn't come out, we knew we had to do something," said McTavish, two giant knitting needles poking from behind his ears.

Madam Lulu admitted she had only pretended to have cramp. "I'm never stuck anywhere, and I never get cramp," she said regally. "What were you doing in his caravan, anyway? What if he'd discovered you?"

Maggie explained how they had been looking for Fozia and the other missing girls.

"Well, I don't know why you think *you* can find them, when we've been looking for them everywhere and found NOTHING!" Rara growled.

"Everyone's been a suspect. Even us. We were accused by the fire-eater of eating them." Dewi swished her tail angrily. "We're vegetarians."

"Me and my brothers were accused of kidnapping them," said Gloomy, on the verge of tears. "We're too busy making people cry. We don't have the time to disappear anyone."

"At first you all thought it was me!" Madam Lulu burst into laughter. "Why would I want to lose someone I've spent hours training, and why would I disappear our boss, Mrs Gumbo?"

McTavish pointed his trunk at AJ, "You accused me of exchanging them for knitting wool. But what about you, AJ? Maybe it's you."

"Don't get narky with me, McTavish," AJ snarled. "If it was me I wouldn't be investigatin' would I? No harm in goin' over the Evidence. A detective never gives up."

"We have to find out who's doing this and stop them

before my latest star disappears like the others," said Madam Lulu, pulling Maggie to her side.

Citra purred "We won't let anything happen to you, will we, girls?" Gloomy held Maggie's hand and McTavish tickled her chin with his trunk.

"It's not just us," AJ said. "I've been told by a chimpanzee just back from Spain that disappearances are happening all around the world – wherever there's magic in circuses, theatres, cabarets, schools of magic."

"One of my uncles disappeared from the jungle with two rats and a python" said Dewi. "They vanished into thin air. He was wearing a gold neck collar. It was priceless."

"Someone somewhere is getting very rich," said Rara.

Madam Lulu looked around at everyone. "Maybe magic is failing. It's breaking up, like smashed china. It no longer has the power it used to."

"There're loads of useless magicians, Brimstone is just one of them. He couldn't magic himself out of a paper bag. Maybe standards are dropping," said Jeffrey and gave Rara a burning look. "Tigers aren't what they used to be either."

"You all know I'm right," AJ said. "Take a gander at this – a One and Two. I found it in Brimstone's caravan."

He waved a small, buckled shoe in the air. Madam

Lulu gasped. "It's Fozia's. She was wearing it the day she disappeared."

"It's a BIG Clue.".

Madam Lulu waved a dismissive hand. "It doesn't prove anything."

"She might have been spying on him, like us, and left her shoe behind," suggested Maggie.

Madam Lulu pursed her lips and AJ shot her a sharp look. "Brimstone isn't as dumb as you think he is."

"As the chimpanzee reported, there've been disappearances of people and valuable stuff from other circuses all round the world – so Brimstone can't be responsible for it all," said McTavish thoughtfully.

"Magicians aren't like they used to be in my day," insisted Madam Lulu. "They used to train for years. Now, they just sit at a desk for one term and then get a certificate at the end of it."

"It's the same with knitting," said McTavish. "Stitches are being dropped all the time."

Maggie stared at the shoe. Wherever Fozia was, someone had taken her there. But who, and to where?

11

"Time to go," yelled Whip-Crack-Away, cracking his whip. It was still dark, but the crew rushed around dismantling the circus. Maggie helped to safely secure the cooking pots, utensils, kettles and crockery into tiny cupboards. Trapezes, hoops, ropes, the high-wire, aerial rigging and costumes were locked into big trunks and placed on a cart to be towed behind the caravan.

The Big Top was emptied and its enormous pegs pulled from the ground. The support poles were removed and the canvas collapsed like a sinking galleon. It was packed away into a tin box barely big enough to contain a pair of shoes. Gloomy looked around him and wept. "It's all over," he said, pulling a sheet-sized handkerchief from his pocket.

"It's a new beginning," said Maggie. "We're going to a new town and you've rehearsed your new act which everyone says is better than the last one. There'll be lots of new people to cry with. You can't keep crying here, people don't want to cry all the time."

Gloomy gave a little sob like a hiccough, wiped his eyes and ran off to find his brothers.

"Let's go," Whip-Crack-Away shouted from his horse.

"Go where?" Maggie asked.

"No idea," Dewi yawned.

"Does anyone know?"

"No. Whip-Crack-Away follows his nose, and we follow him."

"You mean, only his nose knows where we're going?"

"My nose is a wonderful instrument," Whip-Crack-Away said. "It points in any direction you want: upside down, inside out, roundabout and backwards. It's like a compass."

Maggie laughed. "How can a nose know the direction to go? My nose follows me, I don't follow my nose."

"You don't know much do you, little sugar pie?" said Dewi .

"I'm only little."

Rara sidled up to her and opened her mouth, revealing huge, sharp teeth. "I could swallow you in one bite."

"Could you?"

The tiger licked her lips and winked. "We just want to dance with you. There's going to be a party tonight. Fancy coming?"

"Is Brimstone invited?"

"Everyone's invited but he never comes. Thank goodness. He's always miserable."

AJ leapt out from nowhere and landed on Dewi's back.

"Could you please try to land a little more gently. I'm a lady, not a trampoline,"

"Watcha, my old cockrobins," shouted AJ.

"Where've you been?" Maggie asked.

He glared at her. "Searchin' for more Clues, of course."

Dewi gave a low purr, and tipped AJ to the floor before heading to join her friends in the cage. He did not resist when McTavish's trunk caught him round his waist and placed him on his back. Maggie climbed up after him and settled herself behind him. Whip-Crack-Away cracked his whip and his horse set off at a trot into the growing dawn light. Maggie held tight to AJ as the elephant swayed behind the line of caravans. She glanced back at the empty field once filled with tents, booths, performers and excited crowds. Each day took her further away from Josh, and the chance of ever seeing him again was becoming less likely. All around her the tigers sang, while the Grizzling clowns blew their noses like horns; McTavish trumpeted, and AJ screeched tunelessly. Maggie opened her mouth to sing, but her voice was a closed door. Instead, she drummed her feet against McTavish's lumbering sides and tried to think only of breakfast.

Late in the afternoon the circus slowed to a halt and camped on wasteland. Pots were unpacked, campfires lit, horses fed. Performers stretched and exercised, or relaxed in their caravans. McTavish sat with the tigers, quietly knitting and trying to remember who he was while they told stories of their childhoods in Sumatra. Maggie wrapped herself in a blanket and stared into the flames of the fire, listening to Madam Lulu singing in the caravan. She sniffed at the smell of smoke and cooking dinners. Her stomach rumbled. AJ curled up under the blanket with her. His fur was cold and damp.

"Where've you been?" Maggie said.

"A detective's work is never done. I'm knackered." His voice dropped to a whisper. "I've got an Eye Witness Account."

"What's that?"

"It's when someone tells you something they saw. Every detective needs an Eye Witness Account."

"Whose Account do you have?"

"I met one of those parrots we saw in Brimstone's caravan. The one that got away. She said Brimstone tried to do his disappearin' trick on her. She says all of her family has disappeared taking part in his magic tricks. Her dad, her mum, her uncles, her aunts…"

"Does she know where they went?"

"Parrots may be very bright in colour, but not up here," AJ said, tapping his head. "They can't put two and two together. It always makes five. She says when Brimstone put her in the box, she was squeezed as if by a large hand and pulled backwards. It was a struggle to get back. She says she pecked at the lid and flapped her wings. Brimstone opened the box and, Bob's yer uncle, she managed to fly out."

"Poor thing."

"But get this. When she was in the box being sucked back, she heard her family squawkin' for help. She thinks they must be stuck somewhere. She's in a bit of a state. Feels bad that she couldn't rescue them."

Maggie stared into the flickering flames. "Where could they be?"

"I think if they've gone, they've gone for good and there's no findin' them."

"That's not very hopeful. If they've gone somewhere, it means there's a place they can be found."

AJ shrugged his shoulders.

"It's tricky. We'll have to get more Eye Witness Accounts and more Clues."

"What do the audiences think of Brimstone?"

"They think it's funny when his magic goes wrong. They think it's all part of the act."

"Someone is pulling the strings behind all this, as if we are puppets. We have to stop them," Maggie said, pausing to listen to the tigers singing and drumming.

AJ pulled her abruptly away from the fire. "Come on", he said. "Let's go and dance."

12

Josh sat beside Mr Banerjee. He stuck his arm out of the coach window to wave goodbye to Mrs Grubb. He had eaten so much since arriving at Mr Banerjee's he felt sick. He looked down at his new clothes. He was no longer Josh, but a posh boy with shoes that shone and cuffs as white as summer clouds. He was becoming someone he did not know. Mr Banerjee unfolded a map and spread it over his knees.

"We are here, in Random Street," he said, poking a finger at a long line, "and we are heading in this direction." His stubby fingers moved slightly along towards the edge of the map.

"How do you know which direction the circus is going?" asked Josh, having never seen a map before.

"Because a policeman told me, though he didn't know which town they are heading for."

"When shall we catch up with them?"

"Circuses move very slowly so I expect we will catch up with them very soon."

Josh eyed the hamper on the seat opposite them. Mrs Grubb had filled it with sandwiches, cakes, fruit, nuts and lemonade. He asked Mr Banerjee if it would be enough for the journey, and the old man laughed. Josh could not stop eating.

"There's more on top of the carriage and we shall be staying at an inn on the way. You won't go hungry, young Josh."

"Sir, what did Maggie steal from you?"

Mr Banerjee looked down at him. "Something precious."

"I hope she hasn't lost it or given it away," Josh said. "Maggie can be careless at times."

"She would be very foolish if she did. It could be very useful and save her from something very nasty."

"What do you mean, sir?" Josh said, suddenly alarmed. Mr Banerjee ignored him and opened the hamper, revealing a lunchtime feast. After eating, Josh leaned back into the velvet upholstery and fell asleep, lulled by the rhythmic turn of the coach wheels and Mr Banerjee's gentle snoring.

Several hours later he was woken by Mr Banerjee leaning out of the carriage window and shouting at two men, "Excuse me, have you seen a circus pass by?"

The men scratched their heads and gazed down the road. "Yes. It went that way," they said in unison, both pointing in different directions.

"Thank you that was very helpful," Mr Banerjee said, slamming the window shut and urging the coach driver to continue.

"What are we going to do? Everyone is pointing us in different directions. We're never going to find the circus. I'm never going to see Maggie again."

Mr Banerjee unfolded his map again. "We are here," he said, jabbing his finger at a tiny cross on the map and frowning. "When we reach the inn, we'll ask if anyone has seen the circus."

The Inn and Out was warm and cheery. A huge fire blazed in a stone hearth and the innkeeper was a jolly man, with cheeks like apples. His wife brought them plates of roast pheasant and gravy and steaming potatoes. Feeling guilty, Josh resisted licking his lips. "I wish all my friends at the

Scribbens' Home could have a meal like this every day," he said, and licked at the gravy dribbling down his chin. After the meal Mr Banerjee asked everyone at the inn if they had seen the circus. Nobody had.

"What are we going to do?"

"We've reached a dead end. We have to go back."

"But we have to find Maggie." Josh was fighting back tears.

Mr Banerjee looked sad. "The horses need feeding and rest. We'll leave early tomorrow morning."

Josh lay in a small bed in the inn listening to the voices floating up from downstairs. He heard Mr Banerjee telling stories from his travels and wished he could be with him. He thought of Maggie, and hoped she was as well fed as he was and wearing clothes as fine as his. It occurred to him that she might not still be alive. He pulled the blankets over his head and buried himself in the dark. His eyes closed and he drifted into a light, unsettled sleep, only to be woken by the loud banging of doors. Miss Scribbens' voice rose through the floorboards. Josh sat bolt upright. He rubbed his eyes; he must be having a nightmare. He opened the door and peeping out from the landing caught Miss Scribbens darting across the hallway.

"Bring my luggage and be quick about it," she screeched

as the innkeeper heaved her suitcases through the main door. Josh rushed back to his room, locked it and peered from the window. Beneath him, Carry-On preened himself on top of a small black carriage, while the thin, bony horses whinnied impatiently. Josh dressed quickly and stood trembling in the middle of the room, not knowing what to do. If Miss Scribbens saw him, he would be dragged back to the Home. The room turned suddenly cold as if the fire had gone out. He imagined Miss Scribbens oozing through the lock.

Mr Banerjee knocked gently on the door and whispered to him from the landing, "Let me in Josh, there's a good chap." Josh opened the door and Mr Banerjee stepped in, a finger pressed to his lips. "It's your Miss Scribbens and her dreadful bird."

Josh nodded, unable to speak.

"You have to stay in the room until they're gone."

Josh wanted to ask if they were looking for him but could not muster his voice. Mr Banerjee answered him anyway.

"They're looking for the circus. They've been asking everyone, but nobody knows. She seems very annoyed. What a dreadful woman."

Josh shoved his hands into his pockets so that Mr

Banerjee could not see them shaking. "So, she knows where Maggie is. She's dangerous when she's like this, sir."

Mr Banerjee tugged at his moustache. "Banerjee is afraid of nothing and no one."

"What if she sees me?"

"She won't. They'll be gone by tomorrow morning. My coachman told them the circus is heading for Lostways. It's not far from here."

"How does he know?"

"He doesn't. I instructed him to mislead them. Lostways is a thick forest. Anyone entering it always gets lost. Some never come out at all."

Josh resisted an urge to tell Mr Banerjee that he already felt lost. Everything was suddenly unfamiliar. All he had known was the Home. Freedom from it was not as easy as he thought it would be.

"We'll be going in the right direction," said Mr Banerjee. "A boy told me that he saw the circus heading north. Lostways is south – the opposite direction. I asked the boy why everyone was pointing us in different directions, and he said all the adults here have no sense of direction because they never go anywhere. I paid the boy handsomely not to tell anyone else."

The heavy thud of luggage landing back on the coach

rose from the courtyard below. "Don't want to go. Don't want to go," Carry-On screeched

"Do as you're told," Miss Scribbens said, stamping her feet, "We have to find Miss Fever-fingers quickly. My treasure has halved since she left. I am nothing but a poor miserable woman, who, despite being destitute, is rescuing unwanted, wayward children with all the kindness of her heart, but it can't continue without the pickings of that devilish devil-child."

Josh and Mr Banerjee moved closer to the window,

"The boy? The boy?" Carry-On croaked.

Miss Scribbens gave a long low cackle. "Oh, him? We'll find him and when we do, he'll be all yours, Carry-On." Josh shuddered as he watched Miss Scribbens squeeze herself back into the carriage. "Lostways," she shouted to the coach driver and they disappeared into the moonless night.

"Let's hope we never see them again," Mr Banerjee said as he opened the window and sniffed the air. "There'll be fog tomorrow, so we must leave early."

In the morning, Josh stood outside the Inn and Out waiting impatiently for Mr Banerjee to finish curling and waxing his moustache. A faint mist gathered around him, but he could still see the long road that led to nothing but

94

wooded hills. A carriage appeared faintly in the distance. It grew closer. Josh stood transfixed. One of the horses limped and couldn't keep up with its companions. A furious Miss Scribbens hung out of the window waving her arms. The wind carried her poisonous voice towards him.

"Whip that horse. Make it go faster!"

Josh dived into Mr Banerjee's coach, slammed the door and curled up on the floor. He heard shouting and banging as Miss Scribbens' carriage ground to a halt behind him. "We have to change the horse," she said. The innkeeper tried to reason with her but she continued screaming. "I'm not buying a new horse. I don't have the money. You have to replace it."

Josh crawled up to the window and lifted his head. The fog was beginning to settle, but he could see Mr Banerjee pushing past Miss Scribbens. He groaned as her huge hands fastened on his arm. "Excuse me kind sir," she wheedled. "Would you be so kind as to assist this helpless woman, whose kindness to the world deserves to be rewarded by a gentleman such as you. My horse has lost one of its shoes and has hurt its leg."

Josh had never heard her speak so softly.

"I'm afraid not, Madam, but I'm sure the innkeeper will stable your poor horse and find you another," Mr Banerjee said. "And would you kindly remove your disgusting hand from my arm."

"Shoot the horse. Shoot the horse," Carry-On crowed.

"Your horses need feeding, not shooting," Mr Banerjee said, storming off towards his coach. He flung open the door, catching Josh by surprise. Miss Scribbens gawped at the small boy through the thickening fog. Their eyes locked. Momentarily puzzled by his familiar face, Miss Scribbens moved closer.

"Carry-On!" she screamed. "Is this who I think it is?"

Mr Banerjee slammed the door shut just before Miss Scribbens and the crow reached them. The carriage sped off at bone-shaking speed. Josh looked back at the evil pair, all flapping arms and wings and cursing.

13

The circus followed Whip–Crack–Away's nose up and down hills, past fields and the occasional farmhouse. Maggie sat behind him on his horse and gazed in wonder at the passing trees and hedges – she had never seen the countryside before. She felt as if she had landed on the moon.

"Are you sure we're going the right way?" she asked, waving to cows in a field.

"Yes," replied Whip–Crack–Away. "My nose is always right."

"How will you know when we reach the right place?"

"My nose will tingle."

The circus stopped for a rest and the tigers called Maggie over. "We're fed-up travelling. Surely we should have reached somewhere by now." Rara flicked her tail impatiently.

"Whip-Crack-Away will tell us when he knows."

"Well, tell him to hurry up," Citra yawned. "Or we'll have him for breakfast."

Rara and Dewi collapsed into giggles.

"Are you *sure* you don't eat people?" Maggie said, suddenly nervous.

Still giggling, Rara assured her they were vegetarians. McTavish lumbered up to them in a knitted kilt and tartan beret.

"Handsome boy," Citra purred.

"Any more news on Fozia since the shoe?"

Maggie shook her head.

"We should have a meeting," said McTavish and trumpeted loudly with his trunk.

The circus performers and crew sat in a circle and watched as AJ held up Fozia's shoe and waved it. "We now have a BIG Clue and a reliable Eye Witness Account," he said and repeated what the parrot had told him.

"Oooooh," everyone chorused. Gloomy and his brothers sobbed. "Poor parrot losing her family like that. She's an orphan now."

The contortionist looked around at everyone. "Where's Brimstone?"

The fire-eater shrugged his shoulders.

Madam Lulu crossed her arms and stared around the circle. "He probably knows you've been saying bad things about him. AJ told everyone how the magician had taken his hat and turned it into a raining cloud, and how he had disappeared a parrot."

"Everyone makes mistakes," Madam Lulu continued. "You're barking up the wrong tree, AJ."

"Woof, woof," chorused the tigers, collapsing into laughter.

AJ jumped up and down in annoyance. "I'm not a dog."

"You could've planted Fozia's shoe to make it look like Brimstone," Jeffrey suggested.

AJ bared his teeth and hissed at him.

"I was with AJ all the time," Maggie said. "There's no way he could have done that without me noticing."

McTavish looked upset. "Maybe I did it, and I've forgotten that I did. Disappearing someone must be as easy as dropping a stitch."

"Don't be ridiculous, McTavish," everyone chorused.

Whip-Crack-Away's voice rose from the head of the parade. "Let's get moving!"

Jeffrey led the tigers back to their cage and AJ clambered onto McTavish's back.

Very soon they were back on the road. "Is your nose tingling yet?" Maggie shouted at Whip-Crack-Away as he trotted by.

"Not yet, but I think it will very soon."

She drew her head back into the caravan and looked at Madam Lulu, who was pirouetting with a small ginger cat curled up and sleeping on her head.

"Why have you got a cat on your head?"

"Because it helps with balance and keeps the neck straight and strong. If you can keep a cat on your head, you can keep anything on it."

The cat opened one eye and winked at Maggie.

"Try it and see," Madam Lulu said, lifting the cat down. It clawed at her hair and wriggled out of her arms. "Whip-Crack-Away's nose will tingle tomorrow and we shall put up the Big Top."

"How do you know?" Maggie said.

"I know more than you think I do. Let's just say, the time is right."

"Right for what?"

"For your debut performance."

Maggie jumped up and down excitedly. Madam Lulu hugged her, but Maggie pushed her away.

"You said I would see Josh soon, but it's been a long time now since AJ gave him the letter."

"I know, dear," Madam Lulu said, coaxing her hair back into shape. "I'm sorry. We've been so busy rehearsing and training."

"I miss him so much. I want him here with me to meet my friends and watch me flying in the Big Top," Maggie sighed. "Sometimes I don't think of him at all, and then I feel guilty."

"We'll find Josh soon. I promise."

The caravan lurched suddenly as it bounced over cobbles. They fell in a heap to the floor.

"I've made you a promise, and now you must make me one," said Madam Lulu. "You must promise never to go into Brimstone's caravan again with that monkey."

"Why not? You said Brimstone had nothing to do with the disappearances."

"He hasn't. He's not bad, just stupid. I'm sure there's someone else behind all this using Brimstone as a cover, and that monkey is just trouble. Will you promise?"

"I'm not very good at promises. I promised Josh I'd never leave him, but I did."

"You can only do your best, dear thing," Madam Lulu said, stroking the cat.

"If it isn't Brimstone, who is it? It has to be someone in the circus."

"I don't know. Don't trust anyone, Maggie. Not even me."

The caravan stopped swaying and Madam Lulu placed the cat carefully on top of Maggie's head. It curled up and fell asleep.

"Start walking up and down and when you're used to the cat, do a couple of *pas des chat* and then twirl as fast as you can. It helps the spine."

Maggie twirled and twirled. She twirled so fast she thought the cat might fly off. Its claws clamped into her scalp as she lifted off the floor and corkscrewed upwards. The cat flattened against the ceiling and gave a loud meow. Madam

Lulu grabbed her ankles and pulled her down. The cat fell from her head and fled into a corner.

"Bravo, bravo, little one!" Madam Lulu cheered. "I knew you were a star when I first saw you. I'll have to be very vigilant and make sure you don't disappear like the rest."

The circus stopped for the night. Maggie breathed in the cool air and looked up at the stars. She was tired of travelling and training. Her muscles ached and her fingers were blistered from gripping ropes, bars and poles. She stared across at Brimstone's caravan and leaned forward as the door opened and a slight figure stepped outside. It was AJ. He closed the door behind him, stuffed something into his jacket, and scuttled down the steps. Maggie ran indoors and took Brimstone's key from a small bag hanging from a hook. She stared at it, wondering how AJ had entered Brimstone's caravan without it. Had he broken in, or had Brimstone let him in?

14

"It's tingling, my nose is tingling. This is it!" Whip-Crack-Away shouted, slowing his horse to a halt in the middle of a town's high street.

Maggie looked around her. "Where are we?" Nobody knew.

"We are Somewhere." Whip-Crack-Away pointed his whip at a large common surrounded by trees and a pond with ducks paddling on it. "It's perfect. Big enough for the Big Top, water for the animals, and enough people to fill our seats."

By the evening the Big Top and small brightly coloured tents were pitched, caravans and wagons parked, and booths erected. A banner announcing "Mrs Gumbo's Flying Circus" hung skew-whiff above the circus entrance. Large bales of hay were pulled from carts to feed the horses, acrobats stood on each other's shoulders to drape colourful bunting everywhere, clowns painted the ticket booth and canvas flapped in the wind. The Big Top rose above it all.

The townspeople strung bunting across the streets, enjoying the festive atmosphere. Posters were pasted everywhere proclaiming the fabulous acts. Maggie stared at a poster of her with Madam Lulu flying through the air. She ran her fingers under the words, struggling to read them: "Meet the world's only living Cannonball – the Death-Defying Flying Lulu – performing with her miraculously Fast-As-A-Bullet Bird Angel. Once seen, never forgotten." She pinched herself, unable to believe that she was the winged, sparkling creature featured on the poster.

"Where's Brimstone?" McTavish asked looking around.

"He's disappeared," the Grizzling Brothers chorused and burst into tears. The tigers looked nervously around them. AJ volunteered to go to his caravan. "He's probably forgotten it's the parade."

Maggie followed him out of the tent. AJ climbed the steps of Brimstone's caravan and knocked loudly on the door. There was no reply. Maggie looked at him suspiciously. "What were you doing coming out of here last night?"

AJ squinted at her through narrowed eyes so that he

looked more like a cat than a monkey. "You'd make a good detective, Maggie, spying on me like that."

"I wasn't spying. I just saw you. You don't have the key. I do. Brimstone must have let you in."

AJ pulled six balls from his pockets and juggled them in the air. "Brimstone asked me to help him with his magic."

Maggie blinked disbelievingly.

"Why you? You're a juggler not a magician."

"Yes. I'm very nifty with me brass bands," he said, fluttering his hands like tiny wings as the balls sped in the air. He dropped them to the floor and moved closer to Maggie. "I was on a mission to find more Clues. Brimstone admitted his tricks weren't working and I offered to help him."

"How?"

"I helped him rehearse. I held the titfer, he popped a rabbit into it and a couple of mice, covered it with a scarf, waved his wand, and hey presto, they disappeared."

"Did they come back?"

"No, but they did when *I* waved the wand. He begged me not to tell anyone how bad he was. He said he wouldn't know what to do if he had to leave the circus."

"Do you believe him?"

"He's either a hopeless magician or a good actor. I

showed him how to use the wand properly and now he's OK."

"How do you know how to use a magic wand?"

"I'm a detective. You have to know a lot of things, like Clues, Evidence and Confessions," AJ said, picking up the balls and pushing them into his pockets.

"Did you ask him if he disappeared Fozia and the others?"

AJ pulled his tiny notebook from his pocket and read from his untidy writing. "I didn't have anything to do with it. I'm innocent. I did some magic with Fozia but she never disappeared. It's the rabbits, pigeons and doves who have started to disappear." AJ snapped the notebook shut. "Those were Brimstone's actual words. It's what you call a Denial by a Suspect."

Maggie was impressed. AJ really knew how to detect.

"We have to look through the window to see if he's in," AJ said, leaping onto Maggie's shoulders. She walked round to the back and AJ peered through the window.

"It's empty like before. Everything disappears when he's not in it and then, when he is, it's like a proper caravan."

A hand seized Maggie's arm. "You promised me you'd stay away from Brimstone." Madam Lulu pulled AJ from her shoulders and glowering at him.

"He's gone," said Maggie.

"Brimstone? He never misses a parade. He loves the crowds. Where is he?"

They all three looked at each other, unwilling to voice their fears.

"What are we going to do?" asked Maggie.

AJ shrugged his shoulders. "Let's wait and see if he joins the parade. "

Madame Lulu pulled Maggie towards the tent. "He won't. He's with Fozia and the others, wherever they are. We won't see him again."

*

Oompah. Oompah. Thundering drums and clashing cymbals announced the circus parade. It wove through the town, led by dancing horses. Maggie posed with Madam Lulu on a large turntable, revolving in a cloud of brightly coloured sequins, feathered wings and tulle. Six chimpanzees pulled them along, in crimson suits and golden turbans. Crowds drew back in fear as Dewi, Rara and Citra spat, growled and flashed perfectly manicured claws through the cage bars. Jeffrey snapped his bullwhip and growled back at them. The town gasped as McTavish swaying imperiously to the out-of-tune band, while AJ juggled balls of fire on his head. Gloomy and his brothers formed a leaning tower, balanced one upon the other, weeping loudly and waving wet handkerchiefs at the crowd. There were flame-throwers, dancers, horses, contortionists in knots and a band following behind. There was a rush to buy tickets as everyone agreed they had never seen such a spectacular spectacle.

Rara collapsed on her back after the parade and waved a paw in the air. "That was exhausting. It's such hard work being mean."

"Some people love it," Maggie said, thinking of Miss Scribbens.

Whip-Crack-Away walked over to them. "Has Brimstone shown up yet? People have been asking where the magician is. I've had to tell them we don't have one. They've started asking for their money back."

Everyone shook their heads. AJ looked around him. "I can take his place. He says I'm a better magician than he is."

Maggie and the tigers stared at him, seeing him in a new light.

"I don't just throw balls in the air," he said, drawing a wand from his waistcoat.

Maggie gasped. "That's Brimstone's!"

"He lent it to me."

There was a long silence.

"We haven't got much choice if we want to sell tickets." Whip-Crack-Away pulled a fob watch from one of his long-fringed boots, "You have an hour to get ready, AJ. You'll take Brimstone's usual slot, after Madam Lulu and her Bird Angel."

AJ scampered off, chuckling.

In the caravan Maggie's hands shook and beads of sweat broke through her makeup. Madam Lulu dressed her in a silver tutu and spangled turquoise tights. She fixed stars into her hair and strapped wings of bright orange onto her back. She stepped back to look at her. "You look like a bird of paradise," she said, jigging on the spot.

"What's paradise?"

"It's a place where everything is beautiful and everyone is happy."

"I want to go there with Josh, you and all my friends."

Madam Lulu placed her hand over her heart. "You must make your own paradise – in here, Maggie."

Maggie frowned. Sometimes Madam Lulu spoke in riddles.

"Oh, and another thing, my little angel… do you have anything that brings you luck?" She pushed a hand into her bodice and pulled out a small silver star. "I never perform without this. It's my lucky charm. Everyone must have one when they perform."

"I don't have one."

Madam Lulu opened a drawer and held out the stone Maggie had stolen from the old gentleman. It glinted in the light and appeared to throw sparks into the air.

"Tuck it into your bodice, dear. It might bring you luck."

Maggie took the stone and turned it over in her palm. She closed her fingers around it, and felt it beating like a tiny heart.

15

The coach raced at top speed. Mr Banerjee leaned out of the window, his moustache fluttering in the wind like wings. "This is it!" he shouted. "I can see the Big Top."

Josh pulled down the window as they approached the common. Music floated in from the tents. Mr Banerjee shouted at the coach driver to stop. "We mustn't miss the show," he said, jumping out.

"I hope Maggie's here!" Josh said as they rushed through caravans, kiosks, sideshows, food stalls and bales of hay. Mr Banerjee bought two tickets and entered the tent. The circus ring was surrounded by excited faces. Everyone was dressed in their best clothes. They squeezed onto a bench and Josh looked around for Maggie. A gasp, like a gathering wind, rose from the audience as they were plunged into darkness. A thunderous drum roll summoned them to silence. Josh gripped his seat, expecting it to take off at any moment and whirl him through the air.

Flames flared from torches around the ring and Whip-Crack-Away entered, handsome on his galloping horse. He raised his large hat and cracked his whip. Chimpanzees burst squealing into the ring and roamed through the audience, terrifying everybody. McTavish wandered in and performed his tricks, ending up seated on several ringside seats, clicking his knitting needles in time with the band. Josh thought he must be dreaming. Maggie watched from behind the entrance curtain as the Grizzling Brothers rushed past her and somersaulted into the ring ready to flood the tent with tears. "I'm on next," she whispered, trying to sound calm.

"You'll be fabulous, darling," Dewi crooned. "You'll fly like a bird."

"Of course she will, "Madam Lulu said, ignoring the sobbing audience.

"It sounds like a funeral," Dewi grumbled.

Maggie stiffened as Whip-Crack-Away announced their act: "And now, for your delectation – the wondrous, the unbelievable, the death-defying Flying Lulu and her flying wonder, Bird Angel." The crowd dried their eyes and clapped and whistled. Maggie took out the stone, kissed it, shoved it back into her bodice and ran into the ring. The rope dropped and, gripping it tightly, she climbed up to the garlanded platform. Madam Lulu stepped beside her and seized a trapeze. "Good luck my little angel," she said. "You know what to do."

Maggie looked down at the blur of upturned faces. If only Josh were there to see her. Maggie perched on a trapeze bar and watched as Madam Lulu clamped her teeth on a rope that hung above her. She spun from it with such speed she turned into a cloud of whirling, flashing lights. Minutes later she appeared on the other side of the tent, swinging nonchalantly from a trapeze. Josh gawped up at the two small, sparkling figures. If only Maggie were there to see this.

Maggie hooked her knees over the trapeze bar and, upside down, swung backwards and forwards towards Madam Lulu. The stone in her bodice grew hot and pulsed against her skin. It seemed to be pushing her forwards. She dived into the air and reached out to Madam Lulu. The stone shifted inside her bodice, distracting her. She missed Madam Lulu's hand by a fingernail and in less-than-a-blink-of-an-eye fell towards the ring. The audience rose from their seats in horror. Without a safety net there was no hope.

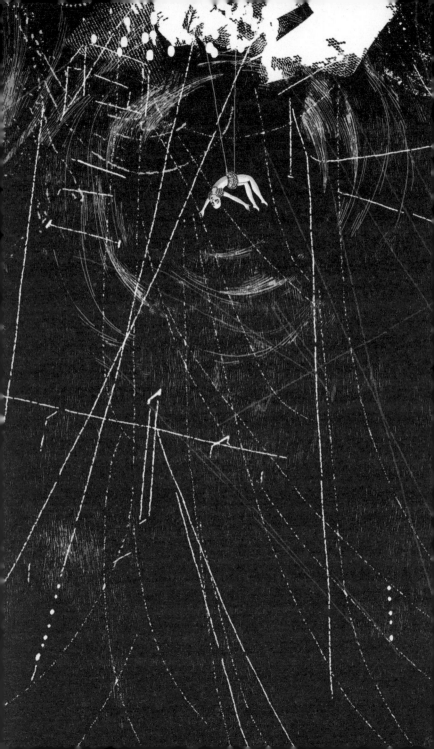

"Not again," McTavish groaned, throwing down his knitting needles and rushing into the ring to catch her with his trunk. The band stopped playing and a heavy silence filled the tent. Maggie's nose hovered over the sawdust, the audience broke into a frenzy of stamping feet and whistling. Her wings suddenly opened in a flash of orange, and like a spark from a fire, she shot up into the air. Josh watched open-mouthed as the winged creature kicked her legs, whizzed around the Big Top, dive bombed towards the ring and twisted upwards in defiance of gravity. Seconds later she was on the platform waving to the dumbfounded crowd below. Madam Lulu stared at her in astonishment. "You're better than me," she cried, and taking her by the hand, they zoomed through the air and landed in the ring. The band struck up again, the crowd roared, hats flew in the air, children screamed. Relieved, Josh sank back into his seat. "A miracle!" Mr Banerjee said, clapping furiously. "Bravo, bravo."

Exhausted, Maggie and Madam Lulu bowed and ran off to shouts of "Encore, encore!"

The circus performers gathered around them in excited admiration. "You were amazing, darling," Citra said, swishing her tail.

"Did you fall like that on purpose?" Jeffrey asked. Maggie winked at him.

"Clever, very clever," said AJ . "Almost magic."

"That's what circus is – magic and dazzle," said Madam Lulu with gusto.

"Come on girls, you're on next. Be as mean and nasty as you possibly can," said Jeffrey to the tigers. They gave a bored sigh and slunk into the ring growling.

Madam Lulu hugged Maggie. "You were amazing, my Bird Angel."

Maggie smiled. "And I'm still here," she said, the stone cooling against her skin.

16

The tigers prowled menacingly around the ring, eyeing the audience. Terrified children clung to their mothers. Jeffrey cracked his whip, and they balanced on chairs, jumped through flaming hoops and wrestled, all the time baring their enormous teeth.

"Thank goodness that's over," Rara said afterwards, ignoring the applause. She winked at Maggie. "We can go and have some fun now, can't we girls?"

AJ draped an oversized black cloak over his shoulders and settled a top hat on his head.

"Good luck," Maggie said.

"Thanks," he grinned. Two chimpanzees passed by, pulling a large colourful box and a cage of subdued birds and rabbits. AJ waved Brimstone's wand under her nose.

"Now for some real magic." He swaggered into the

ring, his cloak trailing behind him. He raised the wand in acknowledgement of the crowd's deafening applause.

"And now for some death-defying magic," he shouted. "I will transport you beyond the realms of belief, and tonight when you are tucked up in your cosy little beds, you will think it was all a dream and only remember the spectacular magical talents of Agent Jackson, the world's one and only Magic Monkey."

Madam Lulu shook her head. "Thinks a lot of himself, doesn't he?"

"He's going to make a fool of himself. Nobody's that good," said Dewi.

With a dramatic flourish, AJ pulled a crimson scarf from a pocket. The audience fell silent. A dove flew onto his arm. He flung the scarf over it and waved his wand. The scarf collapsed. The audience gasped. He rolled the scarf into a ball and threw it into the air. A brightly coloured parrot flew out and settled onto a trapeze. The scarf floated to the floor. The audience looked around them. Where was the dove?

He aimed the wand like a thunderbolt at the neat black-buttoned boots of two elderly women. They screamed as the wand sucked the boots from their feet. The audience watched open-mouthed as the boots floated and swayed above them as if blown by a celestial wind. The leather cracked open and tiny buttons flew into the air. Two enormous wings emerged from each boot, casting shadows across the ring. The boots had disappeared. Instead, four black bats circled the tent like vampires hunting for blood. They finally hung themselves upside down from the tightrope and folded their wings into their bodies.

"Give us back our boots!" the women shrieked.

AJ laughed and shouted at the bats to come down. The drums rolled but the bats remained motionless. AJ pointed the wand at them and their wings slowly unfurled. The women clutched at each other as the bats flew menacingly towards them. "Go away! We've changed our minds – we don't want our boots back," they shouted. The bats exploded in the air with a loud bang. The boots slid back onto the women's feet and they ran out of the tent. The crowd jumped up and down in a frenzy. AJ rushed over to Maggie and pulled her into the ring.

"Let me go," she said, wriggling in his grip. The crowd roared in approval. Josh moved forwards in his seat. Bird Angel looked very much like Maggie.

"Stay still," AJ hissed. "There's more detectin' to be done, so do as I say." He turned to the audience. "And now ladies and gentlemen, prepare yourselves to witness the most audaciously miraculous trick ever performed – with the help of the lovely Bird Angel."

He pointed the wand at Maggie. The circus spun around her like the fast hand of a clock. AJ flexed his fingers and light caught the blade of a sword falling into his hand. He sliced through the air with a flourish and the crowd cheered. Alarmed, Josh watched as the Bird Angel rose slowly into the air.

"It's Maggie!" he cried, clutching at Mr Banerjee's arm.

"Before your very eyes this beautiful creature floats in the air like a butterfly suspended in a fragile web of magic," AJ announced, passing the sword beneath her and around her.

Maggie stared blankly into the distance, unable to move. AJ flung his cloak over her. The sword glinted. "This is a keen and deadly weapon. I stand. I aim. I strike to kill." He ran the sword through the cloak and Maggie. She spun so fast she thought her arms might fly off. Lightning flashed around her, a wind roared, and she felt herself squeezed like liquid through a tiny hole into silence. Her eyes closed and everything disappeared, as if she no longer existed. The audience clapped and cheered. Josh rose to his feet. "No!" he cried.

The cloak crumpled to the floor. "The butterfly has

gone to a land of shadows and secrets," AJ said and, looking around him, added darkly, "In this world nothing is as it seems."

Drums rolled. The audience fell silent. AJ lifted the cloak with his sword and shook it. A cloud of doves flew up to the rigging. Maggie was nowhere to be seen.

Josh ran into the ring and picked up the cloak. It hung limply from his hand. He stared at AJ, instantly recognising him as the monkey that had visited the Home. Madam Lulu ran up to them and wrenched the sword from AJ's hands. "You're a worse magician than Brimstone," she screamed as they struggled.

The audience rose to its feet, ready for another act.

"What have you done with Maggie?" Josh demanded.

"Don't worry. She'll be back. You have to let me finish the act."

"If you don't bring her back, I'll cut you into tiny pieces and feed you to the tigers," Madam Lulu said, brandishing the sword. "Give me the wand."

"You're ruining my act," AJ snarled and lunged forwards to snatch the sword from her.

"Where is she, where's Maggie?" Josh demanded, beating him with his fists. The audience roared with laughter.

"Go away, you're spoiling my magic," AJ said

"She's gone – like the others!" Madam Lulu screamed.

"Wands are only as powerful as those who use them," AJ said, stroking the wand. "It's very powerful now, because I am."

"You're just a little monkey," Josh snorted. "Get her back."

AJ waved the wand in circles and called out for the Bird Angel. A sudden commotion at the entrance of the Big Top made them turn, A shrill voice bounced off the tent's canvas. "Come on Carry-On, follow me."

Miss Scribbens' eyes scanned the audience and settled on Josh like two birds of prey.

"There's that little runt," she screamed, pointing at Josh. "Carry-On, get him!"

The bird swooped into the ring followed by Miss Scribbens. She moved slowly, her skirts trailing and billowing behind her like the wake of a large ship. Carry-On dived at Josh and pecked at the back of his neck. "Where is she? Where is she?" he cawed. The audience cheered.

Miss Scribbens pulled hard on AJ's tail. "Isn't this the vile creature that tried to strangle me, my dear crow?" she sneered.

Balls bounced from AJ's pockets. Miss Scribbens skidded over the balls and fell flat on her back, legs waving in the air like an upturned beetle. The audience roared with laughter at what they thought was a new clowning act.

17

Maggie lay on her back groaning. Her body ached and rumbling thunder filled her head. She opened her eyes. A kitten was licking her ear and a snake slithered over her legs.

"It's you!" a voice said.

Still dazed, she looked up. "Brimstone! What are you doing here?"

The magician held out his hand and pulled her up. She stared around her, sensing she was in a room, yet there were no windows, no doors and no walls. Above her, a ceiling of water ran like a river to nowhere. Rabbits hopped across hummocks of grass and stones. Flocks of birds pecked at the fish swimming in the river. Behind her lay only darkness and a tiny pinhole of light.

"Where are we?"

"Welcome to the Kingdom of Broken Magic. We knew you would get here eventually," Brimstone said, no longer the stately magician. His hat and cuffs were filthy and his moustache hung like washing over his mouth. Maggie threw him a puzzled look.

"This is where all the disappeared come to," he said. "When a magic trick goes wrong, the victims, like you and I, and valuables, such as gold, jewellery, purses, money, all end up in the Kingdom. We are just bits of Broken Magic."

"I don't know how I got here. AJ pointed the wand at me in the ring. After that, I don't know what happened," Maggie said, suddenly recalling the parrot's missing family. Were they in the Kingdom too?

"I've been trying to find a way to get out, but it appears we're sealed in. If we don't know how we got in, how can we get out?"

"There must be a way," she said, and jumped as an enormous, rusted door rose noisily before them. They watched as it slowly opened, revealing a long high hall. Brimstone took her hand and they walked nervously through it, sinking into a floor of floating clouds. Ahead of them, in the centre of the hall, a large colourful crowd gathered. People of all shapes, sizes and colours from all over the world stood huddled together. They spoke in low, frightened voices and their eyes darted nervously about them. A small girl with long black pigtails stepped smiling towards Maggie. "I wore that costume once at the circus," she said. "You're Madam Lulu's new girl, aren't you? I'm Fozia and over there are Alice, Aisha and Loka." Three girls waved shyly at her from the other side of the hall.

Maggie hugged Fozia as if she were an old friend. A tall woman in a brightly coloured turban burst through the crowd. "Brimstone. Is it really you? And who is this? Another Madam Lulu protégé?" She grinned and held out her heavily tattooed arms. "Soon everyone in my circus will be here."

Brimstone tried to hide his embarrassment as she pulled him to her and stood on tiptoe to kiss him.

"Who are you?" Maggie asked.

"I'm Mrs Gumbo of Mrs Gumbo's Flying Circus. Oh, how I miss everyone," she said, tears fattening in the corners of her eyes.

"We don't know how long we've been here," Fozia said. "Time doesn't exist here."

"You've been missing for ages. Everyone is looking for you."

"They won't find us. How can anyone find us?"

Brimstone said and introduced Tearful, the youngest of the Grizzling Brothers.

"I'll never see my brothers again. No-one will ever find me," he said, wringing his tear-soaked cuffs.

Anxiously, Maggie wondered how long she had been in the Kingdom of Broken Magic. Was it years? She might never see Josh or the circus again. But that was impossible! A surge of defiance forced her fist into the air. "We must find a way to escape," she said.

The crowd surged towards her. "Did you say ESCAPE?!" they clamoured. Birds flew down and settled on heads and shoulders. Rabbits, cats and dogs ran between their legs. Escape? Escape? Escape. The word was repeated so many times Maggie felt dizzy.

A young woman in a silver bodice and with ostrich feathers in her hair pushed through the crowd. "Hello, I'm Yui," she said. Maggie stared down at the woman's muscled hairy legs, short red trousers and big black boots.

"Are those your legs? Maggie asked.

"No, they're not," Yui said. "They belong to someone else. I've been looking everywhere for mine. Look out for them please, they're long and thin in blue stockings and buckled shoes. I keep tripping over these hideous feet. I'm not used to them. If you see someone with mine, please let me know."

A man with Strongest Man in the World tattooed on his chest pointed at Yui's legs. "Those are mine!" he yelled and looked down in disgust at his small girl's legs beneath a tutu. "I keep falling over with these when I walk. They can't support my body." He stared at Yui's legs. "I want them back. I'm called Muscles. People will laugh at me with legs like this. They're like pipe cleaners. And I'm stuck with this tutu. I can't get it off."

The crowd surrounding him murmured in sympathy and Yui burst into tears. "You can have them, but I don't know how to give them back to you. I'll have to find mine first."

Maggie looked around at all the mismatched bodies. The thin, folding upper body of a contortionist balanced on the legs of a hefty knife-thrower; a tall, sinuous acrobat hobbled in the heavy skirts of a fortune-teller, while an embarrassed fortune-teller tried to cover unsightly

131

knobbly knees. An Indian snake-charmer, a viper sleeping round his waist, struggled to move in baggy clown trousers and long striped shoes like boats.

"Like everyone here, I'm a magician's mistake," Yui said. "I was asked by a magician to take part in his trick. I was to be sawn into two and would leap out in one piece, shocking the audience. One day the performance went wrong and I ended up in the Kingdom of Broken Magic with these awful legs." She glanced at Muscles and whispered, "Sorry. Nothing personal. I'm sure they look lovely on you."

"That's how I got here, too. I was hidden under a cloak and disappeared," Maggie said checking her body, relieved it was all still there.

"Me too," said Brimstone. "That wretched monkey convinced me he was a better magician than me, and I ended up here. He stole my wand. I feel so humiliated."

"Apparently we have to

wait," Mrs Gumbo said, pointing up at the sign floating above them. It read WAITING ROOM in large letters.

"Waiting for what?" asked Maggie.

"We don't know."

The crowd fell silent.

"There's a Voice that comes from nowhere and tells us what to do. We don't know who it is. It says we are in the Kingdom of Broken Magic and that we shall be here forever," said Mrs Gumbo anxiously.

Fozia cuddled up to Maggie. "How is Madam Lulu? I miss her." She looked nervously in the direction of several snakes curled around a pillar looking for their charmers.

"She's fine. I just hope she doesn't end up coming here," replied Maggie, holding her new friend close.

Brimstone picked up a broken wand from the floor. "A sign of bad luck," he said with a dismal frown.

Nobody moved, each lost in thoughts of the loved ones they might never see again. They didn't notice the reappearance of the door until they heard someone knocking loudly on it.

Mrs Gumbo rushed forward and pushed it open. A small figure stepped into the hall. Maggie stared, unable to believe her eyes.

"Josh!" she yelled and rushed up to him. They clung to each other for a long time.

"I can't believe you're here," she said. "Is it really you?"

"It's me alright," he grinned, surprised at how her skin shone, clean and clear, and how her hair framed her face so neatly. He looked around him, his grin quickly fading. "Where am I?"

"The Kingdom of Broken Magic!" everyone chorused. Josh looked at Maggie as if expecting an explanation, and felt a sudden flash of anger. He stepped towards her and clenched his fists as if ready to box.

"How could you leave the Home without me, Mags? I've been looking everywhere for you. Good friend you are!"

"I didn't mean to. I was rescued from a fate worse than death by Madam Lulu."

"So? Does that mean you had to stay? You promised you'd never leave the Home without me, but you did. You said you'd come back for me. You didn't. I waited but you never came."

Josh's face reddened and he looked as if he might cry.

"I'm sorry Josh," Maggie said, trying to comfort him. He pushed her away. "I wanted to come back for you, but there was this smell of cooking in the caravan and I... I was very hungry. You would have done the same."

Josh nodded and smiled. "I would. I'd do anything for a plate of chips right now. Being here doesn't mean I'm not hungry."

"Do you forgive me?"

"Not really," said Josh sulkily. "I don't think I will trust you ever again."

Maggie grabbed him by the shoulders and shook him. "You can trust me Josh. I would do anything for you. You wait and see."

"Really?" said Josh, turning his back on her.

"Stop the arguing," interrupted Brimstone stepping forward to introduce himself to Josh. "We all need to stick together. It's the only way we shall survive this place."

"Brimstone is right," said Mrs Gumbo. "Unity is strength." She looked directly at Josh. "And you, young man, must learn to forgive."

Josh thrust his hands into his pockets and sulked for a moment before brightening and telling Maggie a little of how he had arrived in the Kingdom. She briefly explained how she had joined the circus but had not forgotten him. "I just needed to be strong to face Miss Scribbens again and get you out of the Home."

She gazed shyly at him. He was taller and his hair was brushed back away from his face. He smelt of soap and he wore a suit with a cravat so that he looked like a miniature gentleman. For the first time in his life, he was wearing shoes, but one thing had not changed – his smile.

"We have to get out of here," he said and shuddered. "I don't have a good feeling about it."

"If this is a kingdom, there must be a King or Queen," Yui said.

"Good point," said Brimstone. "But where are they?"

Everyone looked blankly at each other, waiting for an answer. A deep voice boomed from nowhere, deafening them. "Attention please," it commanded.

"It's The Voice," Brimstone muttered ominously.

"You will all make a line and move towards the Kingdom's Treasure Chamber where you will be given further instructions."

"What does that mean?" asked Yui. Maggie shrugged her shoulders. They watched as another huge door rose before them and opened. Lights glimmered and trumpets blew a loud fanfare, welcoming neat rows of marching monkeys in blue and gold. They prodded people forwards with long pointed sticks and rounded up the rabbits into cages and threw up nets to trap the birds. One of the monkeys dug his stick into Maggie's back. She pushed him away.

"Don't do that again," the monkey hissed. "Or you'll be more than Broken Magic." His companions screeched with laughter.

Josh took Maggie's hand as they walked through the door into a chamber so big there seemed no end to it. Fluorescent mechanical Scoops crawled around on hydraulic spider legs, relentlessly shovelling jewellery, fob watches, tie pins, broken wands, snuff boxes, cigarette cases and coins from the floor into towering mountains. They worked like clockwork with regular, automated steps that crushed anyone in their path. Jewels glittered in the light and watches ticked like a thousand buried hearts. More mountains disappeared into the distance, tiny figures swarming over them like worker bees.

"All this must be coming in from all over the world. It's not just our circus. Broken Magic is everywhere, all ending up in the Kingdom," said Brimstone. "I'm not the only useless magician after all."

137

"We all make mistakes," Mrs Gumbo said as Josh snatched up a hat and placed it on his head. "I'm a gentleman at last," he joked. A monkey sent it flying through the air with his stick and hissed, "Do that again and you're mincemeat."

The Voice boomed again. The monkeys jumped to attention. "From here, you will be taken to the Slumberhall. Once you've eaten the Kingdom's delicious food, you'll be back here to work as the Kingdom's valued miners."

"I don't want to be a miner," whispered Muscles to himself.

"Tough," said a monkey, ramming his stick into Muscles' back. Maggie and Josh followed the crowd. The monkeys led them into a twisting maze of dark, crumbling corridors. Muscles toppled over and had to be carried. Others, who couldn't adapt to their new legs, crawled along on all fours. A light glimmered at the end of the tunnel and opened into a large windowless dormitory filled with never-ending rows of beds.

"Welcome to the Slumberhall," The Voice announced, and, bursting into malevolent cackles, wished them all sweet dreams. Mrs Gumbo collapsed onto the nearest bed and yawned. A clown with the bottom half of a chimpanzee flopped onto another with a deep sigh. Brimstone yawned, pulled a blanket over himself and fell into a deep sleep.

Maggie and Josh found two neighbouring beds, lay back on the pillows and closed their eyes. Soon everyone was snoring.

18

Maggie and Josh woke with a start to the banging of drums. "Wakey, wakey!" The Voice shouted like thunder from nowhere. "Rise and shine. Food is served."

"I could do with some more sleep," Maggie groaned. Trays of dry bread, mouldy cheese and boiled eggs had been placed at the bottom of their beds, along with drab grey work coats.

Gangs of gibbering monkeys ran into the dormitory squealing and waving their sticks. They jumped up and down on the beds and snatched food from the trays. Brimstone pushed one of them away. It jumped back, vicious and screaming, and bit him hard on the hand. Brimstone howled and doubled over in pain.

The monkey flung the work coat at him. "Put this on," he screamed.

Maggie watched as Brimstone slowly buttoned up his work coat with a swelling hand and felt a pang of sorrow. There was nothing more pitiful than a magician who had lost his power.

"I can't eat this rubbish," Josh said, pushing away his tray and thinking of all the lovely food he had eaten since meeting Mr Banerjee. His stomach rumbled loudly. He looked over at Maggie, marvelling at how much she had changed since he last saw her. She was no longer a thin, scabby girl with lice-infested hair. She was taller and stronger, and her hair hung combed and silky to her shoulders, but the sparkle of fierce determination in her eyes and her warm smile had not changed. "Looks like you've been having some good dinners, too," he teased, nudging her.

"Madam Lulu does the most amazing pies, and her cakes are delicious," Maggie said, licking her lips. "Remember how we were always hungry at Miss Scribbens? I never want to feel hungry again." She dug her teeth into the bread and winced. "If we don't escape soon, we'll starve."

"And when is it this evening? Morning and night are all the same."

Maggie tapped her nose. "I'll tell you when," she said mysteriously.

The monkeys herded everyone into a long line. Fozia pushed herself between Maggie and Josh. Tears puddled her eyes. "I want to go home," she sniffed. "I want to go back to the circus." Tearful joined in, and soon everyone was weeping. The monkeys looked on, not knowing what to do. The Voice thundered above them. "Stop this snivelling or you'll be thrown into the Room of Eating Darkness."

The monkeys jumped up and down chattering excitedly. "We'll lock you in there, and the Darkness will eat you up bit by bit."

"Darkness doesn't eat," Fozia said, wiping her nose on her sleeve.

A monkey sidled up to her. "The Kingdom's Darkness does, and it'll enjoy eating you. It'll be so dark you won't see it doing it – but you'll feel it – until nothing of you is left."

The crying stopped and everyone shuffled forwards through the winding tunnels and back into the Treasure Chamber. The mountains rose above them even higher than before and the Scoops were busy delivering yet more treasure to the peaks. The Voice called out again as the monkeys pulled large empty boxes from out of the walls and handed them to everyone. "You will each sort out the Broken Magic and put them into the boxes," it instructed. "Some of you will pick out jewellery, others coins, silver and so on. Anyone caught stealing anything will be sent to the Room of Drowning Tears."

"I think I'd enjoy that room," said Tearful. A monkey stamped on his foot to stop him talking and handed him a big box marked Necklaces. "Start working on that mountain over there. Climb to the top and work your way down."

"What happens to all of this?" asked Brimstone, eyeing a diamond brooch sparkling at his feet.

"I expect it gets sold by whoever runs this place," said Josh.

"They must be very rich," said Maggie, climbing up a mountain looking for earrings. Josh followed, searching for

144

watches. Fozia waved from another mountain, filling her box with key rings.

"There must be a lot of useless magicians in the world," said Brimstone. "And of course, there are the student magicians being taught badly. They must make a lot of mistakes. Like me." His eyes scanned the treasure. "Someone is making a fortune out of this – and us. We're doing all the work, and they don't have to lift a finger."

They worked silently, digging into the mountains with their hands while the Scoops clicked around them. Maggie's back ached and her eyes grew tired. Muscles slithered uncontrollably down his mountain and Yui sank waist-deep into treasure. Brimstone's legs disappeared in a growing pile of coins. If anyone stopped, they were instantly pushed by the monkeys to work faster.

"I don't think we can do this much longer," Maggie whispered to Josh. "People are getting tired."

As she spoke the Chamber suddenly grew darker as if a huge black cloud had passed over. The monkeys looked anxiously above them. "It's going to rain," they screamed. "The cards are coming."

A Queen of Hearts whistled through the air and dropped

to the floor. A deluge of playing cards followed. Spades, Clubs, Diamonds and Hearts whistled through the air, their sharp edges slashing through anything they touched. Monkeys and miners jumped into boxes, burrowed into the treasure or ran into tunnels and waited for the card-rain to stop. When it did, the floor was covered knee-deep in all the card suits. The monkeys emerged cautiously into the Hall.

"You lot," one of them said, pointing to Mrs Gumbo and Yui. "Pick the cards up and put them back into their packs."

"I'm not doing it," insisted Mrs Gumbo, pulling a King of Clubs and a Two of Spades from her turban.

The monkey advanced towards her, glowering; blood trickled down his face and a Three of Spades dangled from his ear. "Are you arguing with me?"

"Yes, I am," Mrs Gumbo said, folding her arms across her chest, preparing for battle.

Maggie and Josh watched as several monkeys surrounded her.

"If you don't do what I tell you, we shall put you in the Room of Drowning Tears," threatened one of them.

"You can put me where you like, matey," replied Mrs Gumbo and kicked one of the monkeys across the room.

Josh dived in and pulled hard on a monkey's tail. Muscles moved towards them but fell over. Brimstone pushed his way into the fray and disappeared in a cloud of cards and monkey fur. Yui kicked out with her big boots. Maggie dived in to rescue Mrs Gumbo, but she had already escaped and was standing alone, watching as the monkeys aimed furious blows at each other.

"I'm taking her to one of the Rooms," one of them shouted.

"No you're not," said another one, punching his neighbour. "I am."

Everyone watched as the monkeys turned into a whirling mass of fur, teeth and tail. Mrs Gumbo roared with laughter, and everyone joined in. They laughed so loudly they did not hear The Voice shouting above them. "The King has blessed us with his return to his Kingdom. All hail to His Majesty."

19

The Voice quashed the laughter and repeated itself so loudly the mountains quaked. The monkeys jumped to attention. An audience with the King was to be held in the Hall of Majesty. His subjects were to assemble to greet him. Trumpets blew and drums rolled, followed by an eerie silence.

"Now?" said Maggie to no one in particular.

"Yes. NOW!" The Voice replied.

The miners put down their boxes and climbed down from the mountains. Figures in polished brass helmets and visors poured into the Treasure Chamber.

"Oh no. Not the Bone Heads," the miners muttered, as the grim figures formed a menacing circle around the Chamber and moved forwards. Even the monkeys were afraid of them. They pushed the miners into rows of five abreast and frog-marched them in a long line through the mountains. A deep rumbling rose from beneath their feet and the floor shook as they moved hesitantly forward. The mountains tipped precariously to one side. Mrs Gumbo's turban slipped off and Yui skidded along the floor. Maggie and Josh clung together with Fozia. Tearful sobbed. The miners fell back as the ground split open before them and widened into a dark chasm. The sound of a great beast crunching on bones rose from the bowels of the earth.

The monkeys herded the miners towards the chasm. Josh and Maggie stared into the darkness and watched as an old rusting staircase wound its way up towards them and settled with a clang at their feet.

"There is no talking in His Majesty's presence unless he summons you to speak," The Voice instructed. "You must bow down before him and not look at him. You must do whatever he tells you to do with a smile on your face. If you disobey His Highness in any way, you shall be punished."

"I bet the King is like a giant wizard, and really frightening," said Josh nervously.

"Those who are mad for power and use it unwisely are small and weak," Mrs Gumbo said. "It makes them feel important and loved. I think, whoever it is, will be very small."

"Loved? Who can love anybody who treats people like this?" said Maggie looking around at the huddle of tired, frightened faces.

"One at a time," the monkeys shouted as they pushed people towards the chasm, and they descended into the darkness, footsteps clanging noisily on the steps in a descent that seemed to go on forever. It could be years before they reached the bottom. Maggie wondered if the circus and her friends would still be where she left them if she ever escaped. She sighed and gathered with the miners in the cold, damp stairwell. None of them knew what to do. An icy mist swirled around them. Suddenly, drums rolled. The monkeys pushed the miners into groups.

"The new arrivals shall lead the procession to the Hall of Majesty," The Voice said. "The King likes to see his new treasure pickers. The rest will go to the back."

"Good," said Josh, pushing to the front. "We'll get a good view of the King."

"Maybe that's not such a good idea," Maggie said, joining him and Brimstone. She glanced back at the others behind her, obscured by the mist.

A loud fanfare split the air. The mist evaporated and the wall ahead of them dissolved into a shower of lights that fell like stars. The monkeys let out a loud cheer. "Our Majesty, our Majesty!" they shouted and pushed everyone forward into the blinding lights.

Maggie grabbed Josh's hand and Brimstone held her arm. "At last, we shall know who rules this place," he muttered.

Momentarily blinded by flames leaping from sconces, the crowd shuffled into the Hall of Majesty and gasped. It shimmered in a blaze of gold. Gold statues, gold carved pillars, gold trees with golden fruit filled the Hall, and its marble floor was studded with shining gold coins. Enormous gold candelabra hung above their heads like exotic flowers. Flags embroidered with magic wands and crowns festooned the walls. The miners gawped, spellbound.

"Someone's doing well," Brimstone muttered.

"I've never seen so much gold," whispered Josh as the monkeys pushed them towards a huge throne of red velvet and carved gilt arms. Monkeys in red and gold stood to attention holding torches of flickering flame. The throne topped a high marble podium guarded by lines of towering Stiltskins. They looked like needles balanced on steel stilts, each eye threaded with a long thin tongue that curled and hissed like water on a red-hot poker.

"Please bow to His Majesty the Supreme Ruler of the Kingdom of Broken Magic," The Voice said reverentially.

High carved doors parted slowly to another fanfare. Necks craned forwards as a small figure entered on a white plumed stallion. A red velvet cloak drowned his shoulders and a jewelled crown fell over his brow. He waved a black and silver wand in one hand and held the reins with another. Monkeys and chimpanzees whooped and cheered behind him. His crown slipped comically further down his face as he acknowledged his subjects with a wave. A Stiltskin helped him to dismount and accompanied him up the stairs. The King threw off his cloak and settled into the throne's plump cushions.

Maggie and Josh froze and stared in stunned surprise. Brimstone's hand flew to his mouth in disbelief.

"Bow before His Majesty you stupid numbskulls," the Voice screamed as a stick fell across Brimstone's back. Knees bent to the floor, heads and backs lowered as the crowd bowed in unison.

"It's AJ," Maggie whispered incredulously. "AJ is the King!"

20

AJ settled back into his throne and the Bone Heads formed an unbroken line between him and the gawping miners. He clicked his fingers. A monkey scurried up the podium with a bowl of grapes. He pushed his crown to the back of his head and addressed the crowd.

"My dear miserable subjects, you're not working fast enough," he said. "There's more treasure to be mined. How do you expect a King to be noble and wise, if he does not have the gold to instruct him?" He twirled his magic wand in the air. The monkeys whooped as if given a signal.

AJ's voice rang in Maggie's ears and she thought she might be sick. He had tricked her all along, pretending he was a detective, when all the time he was using Broken Magic from all around the world to enrich his Kingdom. He had even disappeared people himself, from the circus he worked in! What a fool she had been to have trusted him and his Clues and Eye Witness Accounts. She should have listened to Madam Lulu who was convinced of Brimstone's innocence and thought someone else was guilty.

"AJ tricked us into coming here," she whispered to Josh.

"He pushed me into a box, whacked it with the wand, and I never came back. It was really scary."

Maggie squeezed his hand. A Bone Head moved forward to separate them.

"You may now rise," AJ ordered, popping a grape into his mouth and scanning the front rows. "Let's have a look at the new miners. What a weak-looking bunch." His eyes settled on Maggie with a look of triumph. He pointed to her and ordered the Bone Heads to bring her to him.

They grabbed her arms and pushed her to the foot of the throne. AJ narrowed his eyes and Maggie turned to looked anxiously at Josh. Could this be the last time she would see him?

"Surprised eh, my flying angel?" AJ said in a low voice.

"You could say that," Maggie said. "You really fooled us."

"You must address me as Your Majesty, and yes, you are indeed very stupid. But I like you enough to trust you with a highly venerable position."

"Really? I'm honoured, Your Majesty."

"You shall be one of my Royal Spies and will report any act of treason to me."

"Treason? What's that?"

AJ waited for her to add "Your Majesty".

"That's better. A Royal Spy reports on anyone stealing my treasure, crown or throne or anyone plotting against me. My other spies won't know that you are a spy. You will report directly to me."

"And if I refuse?"

AJ's mouth drew back into a snarl revealing small sharp teeth.

"You'll be thrown into one of the Rooms. I don't care which one," he growled.

Maggie considered the proposal. Being a Royal Spy might be useful for an escape, but it was dangerous. The Eating Darkness would be worse. She knew what Josh would do: he preferred eating to being eaten, especially by the Dark. And so did she.

"Yes. I'll be your Royal Spy... Your Majesty."

AJ gave a dismissive wave. "We shall meet later, to discuss the details. You mustn't tell anyone. I shall know if you do. My spies are everywhere. I shall know every move you make," he said, dropping several grapes into his mouth.

Maggie bowed and turned to face the curious eyes of the crowd. Grim-faced, she returned to her place in the front row beside Josh, more determined than ever to escape the Kingdom.

Despite his protestations, Maggie refused to tell Josh what AJ had said to her.

"But we tell each other everything!"

"I know. When we've escaped, I'll explain everything. You have to trust me."

"That's the problem – I don't."

"Back to work!" a monkey shouted, thrusting an empty box into Josh's hands.

"I can't do this anymore," Muscles wailed. "It's killing me. My legs hurt."

"Then crawl," sneered another monkey.

"I'll stay at the bottom," Muscles said.

"You start from the top and work down," the monkey shouted.

Muscles collapsed onto his knees and crawled slowly up the mountain.

The clink of Broken Magic riches falling into boxes filled the Hall. Monkeys stood guard, flicking their tails and hissing through their teeth. They stashed the full boxes into a corner and shouted at everyone to work faster.

Hands bled from the sharp pins of brooches and tie pins, backs ached, and arms grew tired. Several miners slid down the mountains and tried to scramble back up before the monkeys could attack them with their sticks.

Maggie's hands and eyes were quick from pickpocketing and she worked faster than the others. Soon her box was filled with glittering earrings that had once festooned wealthy ladies. She looked down at Brimstone, struggling to find enough coins. A monkey climbed up to collect her box and gave her a knowing look. Ashamed, Maggie looked around at the miners struggling to meet the demands of AJ's greed.

How could she betray any of them? The stone beat against her chest like the heart of a small bird. She pressed her hand against it. In the Big Top it had made her fly, but did it have the power to help her to escape the Kingdom of Broken Magic? The stone stopped beating and with a sinking feeling she knew it was unlikely.

Josh lay on his bed and stared up at the flocks of birds roosting on the rafters. "Wish I was a bird and could fly away," he said. "You're like a bird, Maggie. You can fly like Madam Lulu. I saw you at the circus. It was like a miracle."

Maggie remained silent and Josh thought she had fallen asleep. She had grown very quiet lately and if anyone spoke to her, she jumped. Her hands were scratched and bleeding, and shook. He turned onto his side with a sigh. Maggie listened as his breathing grew softer. She didn't know how long she had been a Royal Spy, but AJ was waiting for a report from her. She didn't have one, even though two sisters with legs as tall and thin as ropes had wished the King would choke on a bone, and she had seen several miners slyly pocket handfuls of treasure. Was this treason? If she reported them, they would be punished, and she couldn't bear that. Her eyes closed and she dreamt of Madam Lulu reaching out to her as she flew from tree to tree like a bird. She was about fly up to her when someone shook her roughly by the shoulders. "Wake up," a voice hissed. "You have an audience with His Royal Highness."

Maggie rubbed her eyes. A Bone Head stood before her. "Follow me," he commanded and led her through the sleeping bodies. Josh opened one eye as Maggie and the Bone Head disappeared into a small dark tunnel he hadn't noticed before. Throwing on his work coat, he tiptoed after them into the tunnel and followed them up several flights of sumptuously carpeted stairs. Light glimmered from beneath a door where they stopped. The Bone Head looked around him, and Josh flattened himself against the wall. He watched as the door opened and Maggie was pushed into a brightly lit antechamber.

He caught a glimpse of AJ seated at a large table, surrounded by golden candelabra and several Bone Heads. The door slammed shut and he was left in the dark.

Maggie looked across at AJ. Candlelight gave his fur a strange glow, as if he were on fire. His crown and wand lay upon the table.

"You must bow low before His Royal Highness," AJ said.

"I don't want to. You're just a monkey with a crown."

AJ leapt from his chair and onto the table. He rammed his face into hers and snarled, "I would be polite if I were you. This isn't Mrs Gumbo's Flying Circus anymore. I'm the boss here." Something shifted noisily in a corner and an elephant shuffled around the table.

"McTavish!" Maggie cried.

"It's not McTavish. This elephant belonged to another circus, but now she belongs to the Maharajah of Jaipur." The elephant stared sadly at the floor. "I sold her for a lot of money along with a team of stallions. She'll be leaving soon."

"Sold? How?"

"I have a worldwide chain of secret agents who sell my stuff. Broken Magic is making me money. Lots of it. I've got palaces everywhere. It's a growing empire. One day I shall be King of the world!"

Maggie was filled with a sense of foreboding. "How do you get it all out of the Kingdom, Your Majesty?"

AJ thrust his face into hers. "Do you think I'd be foolish enough to tell you how to leave the Kingdom?" He puffed out his chest and strutted up and down the table. "Where's your report?" he demanded.

"I don't have one," Maggie said.

162

"You're a Royal Spy, you must have one. I need to know who is against me, who is stealing from my mountains."

"Nobody is. Your subjects adore you too much to take what is yours," Maggie said.

"You're right," AJ said, smoothing his fur. "I am adorable."

"And you're very clever. You know words like Evidence and Clues."

"Of course. Kings have to know everything, and I do know everything."

"Why do you need spies if you know everything?"

AJ fell silent.

"Knowing is not the same as trusting," he said finally.

Josh pressed his ear against the door and listened in disbelief. Maggie was spying for the King. How could she?

"If I don't have a report from you soon, you'll be punished."

"I'm not afraid of you," Maggie said.

AJ flicked his fingers and the Bone Heads circled her like a pack of wolves. Suddenly the door swung open and Josh fell sprawling into the room followed by a monkey.

"He was outside, listening at the door, Your Majesty."

AJ jumped from the table and stared at Josh.

"Take him," he ordered. The Bone Heads pounced on

Josh and dragged him towards the door. Maggie rushed forwards and tried to pull them off him but they kicked her to the floor. "Where are you taking him?" she screamed as the elephant smacked the table with its trunk and snorted.

"To the Room of Eating Darkness. Say goodbye to your sweet little friend. This is the last you will ever see of him," AJ jeered.

Maggie watched helplessly as the Bone Heads pulled Josh screaming and kicking into the tunnel.

21

Brimstone stared at Josh's empty bed. "Where is he?" Nobody answered. Mrs Gumbo and Fozia peered under beds and looked through cupboards.

"He's gone," Mrs Gumbo said. Tearful sobbed while the miners murmured fearfully amongst themselves, wondering who would be the next to go missing.

"He must have done something very bad," Fozia said.

"Of course he hasn't," Maggie snapped. "Had you, when you disappeared?" Fozia shook her head. Maggie held her hand. "There are those who just like to disappear people," she said darkly.

"Tell me about it," Brimstone said, lowering his voice. "I think Josh has been taken to one of those two dreadful Rooms. We'll never get him back."

"Yes, we shall," said Maggie, struggling to button up her work coat.

"But how?" asked Tearful, his collar and cuffs soaked in tears.

"We must find out where the Rooms are."

Two monkeys walked towards them. They fell silent and returned to their beds. Brimstone stared dismally at his breakfast.

"Be on the same mountain as me," whispered Maggie under her breath, trying hard not to think of Josh alone in the dark and frightened.

"Come along, you lot!" the monkeys shouted, herding everyone out of the dormitory.

Unnoticed, Maggie stood behind them.

"The sooner we get them working, the sooner we can have a break," one of them said to his companion. Maggie leaned in closer.

"We're not having a break. A lot more Broken Magic has arrived in the Kingdom and is in the Waiting Room. It's going to be processed today."

"As if we haven't got enough of them. Vermin the lot of them. Failures. Broken. If you ask me, the King is far too nice to them."

"There's so many – some will have to be let in while the

others are still working. The rest will be allowed in while everyone is sleeping. Reinforcements are being sent to help us out."

Maggie pushed her way past them to join Brimstone and looked around her to make sure no one was listening. She repeated what she had overheard.

"It's going to be chaotic. There are lots more people coming into the Kingdom," she whispered.

Before he could reply, Brimstone was carried along with the miners like a stick in a river's current.

The mountains were bigger than ever, as if while they slept, a flood of Broken Magic had poured into the Hall. Broken wands lay scattered around the floor and flocks of canaries flew in bright yellow clouds above them. Brimstone followed Maggie up a mountain. They dug their hands into its sides, searching for treasure. Yui passed them, her strong legs and boots biting into the mountain's side until she reached the peak. She looked down on them and waved. "There are some advantages to having these legs," she said, opening her empty box.

"No talking!" a monkey shouted up at them.

Maggie pulled out a few coins from her mountain. Yui moved closer to them and watched as Maggie handed them to Brimstone. Could she be a spy? With a sigh Maggie continued filling her box, wondering if she could trust anyone. A picture of Josh disappearing into the mouth of the Eating Dark rose before her, cut short by the wail of a siren. The miners stopped work. Uniformed monkeys rushed in from all sides. Huge gates rose up in the Hall and slowly opened. The new arrivals emerged stunned and tired from the Waiting Room. They shuffled into the Treasure Chamber, staring around them as if in a dream.

"Welcome to the Kingdom of Broken Magic," The Voice boomed. "You shall be known henceforth as miners, and will be briefed as to what you are to do."

The other miners could only smile sadly at them from the mountains. A loud, shrill voice came from the back of the crowd. "Let me out of here, you pile of rubbish. Who do you think you are, keeping me here? I don't care what Kingdom this is. You have to let me out."

Maggie stared in disbelief as Miss Scribbens pushed and poked her way through the new arrivals. Her flounced skirts had been replaced by a pair of knobbly legs in ill fitting tights and scuffed boots with broken heels. Carry-On flew behind her, pecking at the other birds. Maggie stifled a laugh as Miss Scribbens stopped and stared at her.

"Carry-On, it's her! That pocket delver, bringer of

trouble," she screamed and thrust her face into Maggie's. "We were told we would get 20 guineas if we got into his box. Where are the 20 guineas? I have been short-changed. We would just disappear for a minute and that monkey would pretend to saw us in half and then we'd leap out of the box in one piece. The crowd would cheer and clap and we would be famous. We got in and everything went black, there was a sucking noise, and now we're here in this awful place and I am dreadfully changed." She gazed in disgust at her newly acquired legs, unaware that she was surrounded by hundreds of equally strange, mismatched bodies.

"You must bring me my legs and bottom back!" she said, pushing at a monkey, "I am the mistress of the Scribbens' Home for Very Wayward Children and must be released immediately. I demand to see whoever it is who runs this place."

"Call the Bone Heads, this one's trouble," the monkey said, alarmed by Miss Scribbens' flashing fingernail and Carry-On's stabbing beak.

"You can't keep us here," she said, looking around her, noticing the mountains for the first time. Her eyes lit up. "Look at this, crow," she said breathlessly. "Treasure. Tons and tons of gold and silver and trinkets. More than our clever Miss Fever-fingers here could pick in a lifetime."

"Tons!" Carry-On croaked and flew to one of the mountain peaks, returning seconds later with a diamond necklace dangling from its beak. A Bone Head grabbed the bird by its neck and another threw Miss Scribbens over his shoulder. "Get your filthy hands off me!" she cried, trying to kick with her new legs. More Bone Heads arrived. In the confusion, the miners punched and kicked the monkeys, who fought back with their sticks. The siren wailed again and The Voice boomed above it, but no one was listening. A battalion of armoured chimpanzees surged into the Hall and drew their swords. Everyone stopped. The Bone Head carried Miss Scribbens over his shoulders into the tunnel, followed by the other new arrivals.

"Do you know those dreadful people?" asked Brimstone, turning to Maggie. But she had gone. He had not noticed her escape in the confusion of punching and kicking limbs and slip into the tunnel.

Her footsteps rang against the tunnel's stone. Burning torches threw out a stifling heat and she choked on the thick musty air. Sweat stung her eyes, slowing her down. There *had* to be another tunnel leading to the Room. Her legs grew weak, and she leaned against the wall panting, suddenly alone and vulnerable. The thunder of marching boots and the click of stilts vibrated through the tunnel. Bone Head helmets and the Stiltskins' needle heads glinted ahead of her. Resisting an urge to turn back into the Treasure Chamber, she continued running towards the dark shadows of reinforcements. Her eyes searched frantically along the walls for somewhere to hide. A tunnel unexpectedly opened up ahead of her like open arms. She dived in and flattening herself against the wall, waited for them to pass. Peeping out, she saw the last of the Stiltskins disappear and the tunnel fell eerily silent. With a sigh of relief, she inched her way along the unlit tunnel. Her foot caught on the edge of a step and she shot headfirst down the stairs and landed with a bump on the cold stone floor. She lay in the dark, bruised and retching on a thick smell of mould and damp. The faint echo of slurping, chewing, munching and crunching rose around her. Hauling herself up, she felt her way along the tunnel's icy walls. The slurping grew louder.

"Josh, where are you?" she whispered. Time was running out. If she didn't find him soon, he would be gobbled up. Her fingers caught on a hinge and met the smoothness of polished wood. It felt like a door, but she could find no handle or lock. The slurping and munching grew louder, accompanied by faint screams.

171

"Josh, if you're there, answer me!" Maggie shouted, striking the door with her knuckles.

The tunnel fell silent. She banged frantically on the door and pressed her ear to the wood. Someone groaned, "Maggie, Maggie." She pushed hard against the door.

"Mags, the light is going, and the Dark is coming to eat me. It's almost here. I can feel it," Josh whispered weakly. "Please hurry."

Maggie stepped back and hurled herself against the door, but it would not budge. She tried again.

She stood still for a moment, not knowing what to do. Something grew warm against her chest. "The stone!" she cried and reached into her bodice. It lay in the palm of her hand, glowing like a tiny ember. If it could help her fly, surely it could help her open the door? She pressed it against the wood, but nothing happened.

"Hurry, please hurry!" Josh wailed. "Something nasty is licking my toes."

"Open the door please open the door," Maggie begged the stone. It grew cold and lost its glow. In a fit of anger, she threw it on the floor, "Useless... stone!" she cried. Sparks flew as it hit the floor and the door split in two with a loud crack. Maggie picked up the stone and rushed into the Room. The door sealed itself behind her and the

172

Dark pressed against her like a falling wall. She heard it beneath her smacking its lips and chewing noisily as if feasting on bones.

"Josh!" she screamed. "Where are you? I can't see you."

"I'm here," Josh said from somewhere nearby. A loud slurping filled the Room. "Help me! It's sucking my fingers."

The stone remained cold in Maggie's hand.

"I don't know what to do", she said, but suddenly she remembered how it had worked in the Big Top. She pushed it back into her bodice and pressed it against her skin. It beat gently against her heart and grew warmer. A tiny pinhole of light appeared before her, floating like a firefly.

"There's a light, Maggie," Josh said.

The tiny light expanded as the stone grew hotter. Josh moaned weakly, "The Dark is still eating me."

The light grew and beamed into the Dark. Josh's face floated before her. She reached out to touch him but he disappeared. Something licked at her fingers, slurping and gulping noisily.

"Shine the light on my feet and hands before they're gone," Josh begged.

Maggie closed her eyes and imagined swooping and looping through the air. "If you can make me fly, you can bring light too," she said to the stone, pressing it against her skin. She felt it twitch, and then crawl slowly out of her bodice like a beetle.

"It's moving. The stone's moving."

"I hope it's not leaving us."

The stone fell to the floor with a loud crack. A flash of blinding light sliced through the Dark.

"Quick. Let's go," Josh said, snatching up the stone and grabbing Maggie.

The Dark gulped and retched and hurled them against the door. Light filled the Room. The door swung open and closed behind them with a deep sigh. They ran into the tunnel as fast as they could.

"I have to get back before they notice I've gone," Maggie said. "And you have to hide, Josh. AJ will think you've been eaten by the Dark. He won't know you've escaped, but if you're seen, he'll throw you back in there."

Josh shuddered. "The monkeys are everywhere," he said, wiping the Dark's dribble from his hands and face as they ran.

"There are spies everywhere, too."

"Yes, and you're one of them."

Maggie stopped running. Josh faced her. "How do I know I can trust you?"

"Because I've just rescued you."

Josh looked shamefaced. "I just don't know anything anymore, Mags."

"I can use being a Royal Spy to get us out of here. It means AJ trusts me. But first, we have to find you a safe place to hide."

"In one of the empty boxes?"

"Good idea! But you have to be careful. Scribbens and Carry-On are here."

"Oh no! AJ must have Broken-Magicked them here, like he did me," said Josh, and added with a grin, "I bet they love the treasure."

They continued running through the tunnel. Josh would hide under a bed in the Slumberhall, and at night he would creep into the Treasure Chamber to hide in one of the boxes. "You'll have to smuggle some food to me. Something's been eating me but I haven't eaten anything for what feels like a long time."

A voice rang out in the distance. "Spread out. We'll find soon find her."

"It's the monkeys. They've discovered I'm missing," Maggie said. Josh grew pale. He grabbed her hand and, running into the main tunnel, headed towards the Slumberhall. He crawled under the beds and Maggie flung herself onto one of them, clutching her stomach. The monkeys burst in and ran over to her. They pulled her from the bed and she groaned, "Don't touch me. I have a dreadful illness and you might catch it."

The monkeys loosened their grip.

"It's that terrible food you give us. It makes me so ill. I'm going to die," she wailed as if in agony.

"Too bad," a bald monkey said. "You still have to work."

Another monkey sidled up to him. "She's one of the King's Spies. Go easy on her."

The bald monkey stepped back. "OK, we'll come back later."

The monkeys turned on their heels and left Maggie writhing on the bed.

"That was close," said Josh, emerging from under a bed.

22

Aware of Josh hiding several beds away and Miss Scribbens snoring on the far side, Maggie hardly slept. She could tell no one about Josh – not even Brimstone. He might be a spy too. In the morning they were woken by the noisy delivery of their breakfasts. Maggie hid bread and cheese in her pocket and, pretending to look under her bed, scanned the floor for Josh. He had gone. Brimstone eyed her suspiciously. "What, or who, are you looking for?"

"Thought I saw a mouse."

"I'd rather eat a mouse than what they give us," said Mrs Gumbo. "I've lost a lot of weight since I've been here. I keep dreaming of fish and chips and mushy peas."

Miss Scribbens hurled a piece of bread across the room. It fell like a stone at Maggie's feet. "I'm not eating this muck," she said. "I'm famous for my generosity and kindness towards waifs and strays, unlike that mean and cruel child over there." She pointed at Maggie and, turning to the monkeys, demanded that she be brought buttered toast and jam.

They collapsed into laughter and threw a work coat at her.

"I'm not wearing this ugly monstrosity. I've seen better coats on dead donkeys. A lady such as I wears nothing but the best. This is for common workers."

A monkey walked menacingly towards her, swinging his stick. "You are a common worker and a servant of the King," he said, prodding her. "Put it on. It'll hide your pretty legs." The monkeys snorted derisively.

The miners marched to the Treasure Chamber and looked wearily at the growing summits. There was so much Broken Magic, it was never ending. Maggie gazed across at the huge pile of empty boxes resting against the wall. Was Josh hiding in one of them, or had he been captured again? The monkeys handed the boxes to the workers. Miss Scribbens took hers and stared up at the sparkling mountains "It's paradise," she drooled, scratching her nail through the treasure like a rat. Maggie watched as she gave Carry-On a sly look. Hypnotised by all that shone and glittered around them, they did not notice her following them up the mountain.

The Voice boomed out across the Chamber, "To all the new workers – anyone stealing treasure from the King will be severely punished."

Miss Scribbens cackled as she ran her fingers through the treasure. "Pearls, diamonds, sapphires… we could live on a box of these for the rest of our lives, Carry-On," she said, holding a pearl necklace up to the light. "This would look divine on my perfect neck, wouldn't it?" The bird eyed her with approval and picked at an emerald necklace for her box. Neither noticed Maggie sidle up behind them.

"Miss Scribbens," she whispered. "Why don't you put some in your pockets? Everybody does it. When we escape, you will be rich."

Miss Scribbens gave her a poisonous look. "Mind your own business, Miss Nothingness. Miss Scribbens does what Miss Scribbens does."

"I'll make sure no one sees you."

"Will you?" Miss Scribbens stared at her coldly.

"I am a servant of the King and he trusts me. Be ready to take whatever you want just before we return to the Slumberhall. I will give you a signal – a nod of the head. You will have to act fast, though."

A monkey climbed towards them, crunching through the treasure. "Enough of the chat you two. Get on with the picking."

Maggie climbed further up the mountain wondering how she could find Josh. Madam Lulu said she should always have a Plan and she thought she and Josh had one, but it was falling apart. Loud sobs rose above the heavy clink and crash of treasure. Maggie looked across at the neighbouring mountain. Fozia was crouched halfway up it staring at her hands. "My hands are bleeding," she said and held them up. Blood soaked into the sleeves of her work coat. "I can't do this anymore."

Another voice joined her from the summit of another mountain. Soon, hundreds of miners were throwing down their boxes and waving raw, scratched hands in the air, shouting, "We've had enough!" They threw down their boxes and stopped working.

"We want gloves!" Maggie shouted. A heavy silence filled the Hall. The monkeys looked at each other in bewilderment as more voices joined in the chorus for gloves.

Maggie raised her fist and punched the air. "We want gloves! We want gloves!" she shouted. Miss Scribbens and Carry-On looked up at her. Maggie gave them a slight nod and suddenly hurled herself down the mountain. Bits of Broken Magic flew into the air as she gathered speed, knocking over Miss Scribbens and her crow. A group of monkeys watched her roll to the foot of the mountain as everyone screamed, "We want gloves!" Bone Heads poured into the Hall. Unnoticed, Miss Scribbens and Carry-On filled her pockets and underwear with treasure until she could hardly move. Two Scoops moved ominously and mechanically towards the mountain.

A hand clamped tightly around Maggie's arm. "The King has given orders that you come with me," a Bone Head said from behind his mask. The monkeys and the rest of the Bone Heads fell back.

"I'll take her. You've got enough to do with this lot," the Bone Head said gruffly and watched as his colleagues and the monkeys stormed the mountains and dragged the miners down. Maggie offered no resistance. This was exactly what she wanted, although it hadn't been part of the plan. Maybe plans had minds of their own. The Bone Head remained silent until they entered the tunnel. He looked around to make sure they were alone before pulling his visor down.

"Josh!" Maggie burst out laughing. "I thought you were in one of the boxes."

Josh grinned. "Don't I make a great Bone Head? You thought I really was one, didn't you?"

Maggie, who didn't like to admit to being fooled said, "Not really, I thought you were a bit small for a Bone Head."

"Liar. It's not about height. It's about authority. You have to behave like you're the boss. I had them all fooled as well as you."

Maggie looked at him quizzically. "How did it happen?"

"I crept out while you were all sleeping. I wanted to find somewhere to hide but it was impossible. I found some steps and crept down. A Bone Head had taken his helmet and visor off and was fast asleep. I hit him with his stick and took his uniform and hey presto, here I am, Bone Head Josh at your service."

"We don't have much time. We have to find the Hall of Majesty."

A monkey ran breathlessly towards them. Josh and Maggie pretended to struggle. "Sorry, I can't help you mate," the monkey said running past them. "There's big trouble with the miners."

Josh called after him, "Where's the Hall of Majesty?"

"It keeps moving around, but right now, I think it's straight on. Just keep going."

"Thanks. Good luck," said Josh as the monkey disappeared around a corner.

The heavy thud of sticks on skulls and screaming grew fainter as they ran on. They continued until a huge gold door rose before them as if activated by their footsteps. It opened unprompted with a deep sigh. AJ was sitting upon his throne, surrounded by peanut shells and grape pips. He watched as they moved towards the throne and bowed.

"I was expecting you," he said to Maggie. He glanced down at Josh from the podium and ordered him to stand behind the throne until summoned. He beckoned Maggie to join him. He offered her some peanuts. She shook her head.

"Enjoying our food, are you?" AJ gloated. "Not like Madam Lulu's cooking is it?"

"Your Majesty, let's get to the point. I have information on two of your subjects," Maggie said.

"Only two?"

"Yes, two of your newly arrived workers have insulted your Royal Name and are at this very moment inciting the workers to insurrection. They are also stealing treasure."

AJ bared his teeth and hissed as Maggie continued. "I believe you Broken-Magicked them into the Kingdom yourself AJ... I mean Your Majesty."

"Aah, those two," AJ said and clicked his fingers. "Bone Head, is this all true?"

Josh stepped from behind the throne and bowed.

"Yes, Your Majesty," he said, his voice muffled by the visor. "Everything your Royal Spy says is correct. She pointed them out to me, and I witnessed them stealing the treasure. The workers are also restless. I came to tell you immediately."

AJ cracked open a peanut shell and smiled. "We'll have to teach them all a lesson, won't we?"

"Your troops and guards are already there. The situation is under control," said Josh.

AJ reached down under his throne and pulled out a pen and a piece of paper. "What are the names of these traitors?" he asked before scribbling hastily and signing the paper with a flourish. "A Royal Decree," he said, handing it to Josh. "It gives you authority on my behalf to arrest Scribbens and her bird and get rid of them." He popped a peanut into his mouth. "Put that crow in the Room of Eating Darkness and the woman in the Room of Drowning Tears. Now go!" He pulled his wand from under his cloak, scratched his back with it and watched Maggie and Josh disappear through the door.

23

"I'm going to enjoy this," Josh said, a broad grin under his visor, but Maggie knew he was just as nervous as she was. She smiled bravely as he marched her towards the mountains.

The chaos they had left behind had transformed into order and silence. Snarling monkeys pressed the miners against the walls. Brimstone stared across at her with frightened eyes. Mrs Gumbo stood next to him, visibly trembling and holding Fozia's hand. Muscles swayed on his delicate legs, his hands pressed tightly together as if in prayer.

Josh pulled Maggie towards a group of Bone Heads. "I am back from an audience with His Majesty," he said in an authoritative voice. The Bone Heads jumped to attention. "There are two traitors in this Hall, and the King has issued instructions for their immediate arrest and for them to be eaten by Darkness or drowned in Tears." He held up AJ's scribbled orders. The Bone Heads clustered around to read it.

"It's the King's writing alright," one of them said. "Scribbens and her bird, eh? So, that trouble-making, miserable couple are traitors and thieves. Let's get them."

The Bone Heads and monkeys fanned out across the room, peering into every face that lined the walls.

"They've gone!" they shouted across at Josh.

"They can't be far," said Josh.

"The mountain!" Maggie cried, struggling to climb towards where she had last seen them. But there was no sign of them. They had vanished into thin air. Josh and the Bone Heads followed her.

"Maybe they're hiding in the boxes," Josh suggested, sweating heavily under his helmet.

"They wouldn't fit into any of them," Maggie said, climbing further up the mountain. She paused.

"Did you hear that?" she said, looking around her.

"What?"

They stood still and listened. A muffled groan rose from inside the mountain.

"They're hiding in the treasure," Josh said. "Start digging."

The Bone Heads shovelled into the treasure. The moaning grew louder. A large arm ballooned from the mountainside and a long fingernail snapped at the air like a serpent's tongue. The mountain trembled as a red, scratched and bleeding head burst from the treasure and stared up at Maggie. Trinkets of all kinds festooned Miss Scribbens' hair, and tiny beads filled her nostrils.

"Get me out of here," she spluttered, spitting coins from her mouth.

"You look ridiculous!" said Maggie, laughing at the spindly legs crashing through the treasure. "I want my legs and skirt back!" Miss Scribbens wailed.

"Where's Carry-On?" asked Josh. "It must be here, too. It's never far from Miss Scribbens. Keep digging."

A pair of black bird legs wiggled in the air and Josh pulled at them. Carry-On emerged squawking wildly and flapping its wings. It tried to fly off but was held down by the weight of a charm bracelet around its neck. The mountain suddenly quaked and its peak listed dangerously to one side. An avalanche of treasure fell towards them with a thunderous roar.

"Run!" screamed the Bone Heads.

The mountain doubled over and crashed around them like a great sea in a storm. Maggie and Josh fell backwards and hurtled down the mountain with the Bone Heads. They hit the floor in a tangled heap and lay buried in the treasure as it fell all around them. Several Scoops headed towards them, lowering their heavy jaws. Maggie struggled to sit up but was held down by a knot of arms and legs. Josh had been thrown across the Chamber and saw the Scoops moving like clockwork, ready to crush anyone in their path. He adjusted his helmet and visor and pulled Maggie up from the floor, dragging Miss Scribbens along with him. Carry-On's beak poked out from beneath a pile of Bone Heads. The Scoops towered over them. The Bone Heads scrambled to their feet and jumped aside. Carry-On flew into the air. Josh and Maggie looked around alerted by a deadly silence. The Hall was empty.

"Where is everyone?" Maggie said, bewildered.

"They probably escaped into the tunnel when the mountain started to fall," Josh said. The Bone Heads stared gormlessly around them, not knowing what to do. Carry-On glided towards the tunnel, feathers falling from its wings like darts. Miss Scribbens wrenched herself from Josh's hand and ran after the crow, listing on her high heels. Josh, Maggie and the Bone Heads chased after them.

"They won't get far," shouted Maggie. "They'll hit the crowd of people in the tunnel."

But there were no crowds: the rattle of the Bone Heads' helmets and the thud of their boots echoed through an empty tunnel.

Maggie pressed her hand against her chest and felt for the stone as she ran, hoping it would inspire her to think of a new plan. But first, she had to catch Miss Scribbens and Carry-On. She could see them ahead of her: Miss Scribbens limping along with Carry-On hitching a ride on her shoulders. Josh ran forwards and seized Miss Scribbens. A Bone Head grabbed Carry-On by its neck. Maggie breathed a sigh of relief.

"We have orders from His Majesty the King to arrest you," Josh said and, looking around, asked for a pair of scissors.

One of the Bone Heads pulled a pair from his boots. He snapped them open and shut against Miss Scribbens' nose.

"Cut her fingernail off," Josh ordered, savouring his new-found authority.

The Bone Head seized Miss Scribbens' hand.

"No, no, not my nail," she cried. "It took years to grow.

I can't do anything without it. Carry-On, don't let them do it."

But Carry-On could do nothing. He dangled helplessly from the Bone Head's hand like a handbag; Maggie and Josh watched in silent glee as the fingernail clattered to the floor. She had used it and Carry-On as weapons to intimidate and terrorise. Without them, she was stunted and harmless. She stared at her hand and howled at Carry-On, "Useless bird. How could you let them do this to me?"

"Well done," Josh said, slapping the Bone Head on his back. "I shall report this to His Majesty. He'll be very pleased with you. I shall ask that you ALL be rewarded."

The Bone Heads sniggered and grinned behind their visors. Josh took the scissors and shoved them into one of his pockets. "Let's take them to the Rooms," he said.

The Bone Heads marched Miss Scribbens and Carry-On to the Rooms. Maggie followed.

"Throw it in," Josh ordered when they reached the Room of Eating Darkness. The Bone Head threw Carry-On through the door into the waiting Dark. The sound of wildly flapping wings and the licking of lips echoed around them.

"Carry-On, don't leave me!" screamed Miss Scribbens.

"He already has and won't be coming back. You're going

to find out what it's like to be truly alone and at the mercy of something as cruel as you," said Maggie.

"Snivelling brat. I never liked you. The only thing you were good for was thieving," Miss Scribbens said as the Bone Heads pulled her into a narrow, dark tunnel. Josh and Maggie followed. Water trickled down the walls and pooled on the stone floor.

"Off you go," one of the Bone Heads said as the tunnel wall dissolved into a curtain of water. He pushed Miss Scribbens forwards. She struggled to free herself from his grip. "What's going to happen to me?" she wailed. Water gurgled loudly, as if plunging down a sink hole.

"You're going to drown in all the tears you never shed," said Josh.

"The King won't stand no nonsense from anyone," a Bone Head sneered.

"I can't swim!"

"Too bad," the Bone Heads chorused and pushed her through the water. She disappeared with a loud splash and the wall turned back to stone.

Maggie and Josh glanced at each other disbelievingly. The impossible had happened: Miss Scribbens and her crow were gone forever.

24

Maggie and Josh burst into the Slumberhall, followed by the Bone Heads. Frightened eyes peeped out from beneath shelters of hastily piled mattresses and pillows. Monkeys clung to each other under jumbles of iron bed frames. Brimstone shoved a dishevelled head out from one of the shelters. "Is it safe now?"

The Bone Heads nodded in unison. The miners emerged cautiously from their shelters, brushing fragments of treasure from clothes and bodies.

"Sweep it up," the Bone Heads ordered. Brooms appeared from nowhere.

"She's not sweeping," Josh ordered, as a monkey thrust one into Maggie's hands. Josh pushed it back. "She has an audience with His Majesty and I am escorting her to His Royal Highness." Everyone, apart from the miners, knew that she had been promoted to Chief Spy. He turned his back on them and escorted Maggie out of the Hall.

Brimstone stared after them, thoughtfully tugging at his moustache.

Once safely outside the Hall, Josh shared his fears with Maggie that the Bone Head whose uniform he had stolen might soon be discovered.

"What shall we do?" he whispered in despair.

Maggie shrugged her shoulders. Things were getting complicated. "We have to act quickly before they find out, or we'll end up like Miss Scribbens and Carry-On."

"We're not very good at escaping," said Josh, reminding her of their failed escape attempts from the Home.

"Madam Lulu says you must always have a plan. I'm working on one, Josh. It will be risky, but it will get us all out. I promise."

"If we don't know where the exit is, we can't escape. I didn't come in through a door. I don't remember anything about entering the Kingdom. AJ shoved me into a box and I woke up in the Kingdom, with a river over my head and a tiny pin of light behind me. Only AJ knows how to get in and out…"

"…with his wand!" they chorused, and raced down the tunnel towards the Hall of Majesty. Its doors rose before them, revealing the Hall's royal dazzle of gold. They blinked and stared at the empty throne.

"Where is he?"

As if in answer to Maggie's query the Voice broke into the room, "His Majesty is waiting for you in the Royal Salon. Follow the Path to Ruin." The Voice burst into maniacal laughter.

A path of black crystals appeared beneath their feet like a glittering serpent. "I don't like the look of this," Josh whispered. "Ruin is not a good word." They set off down the never-ending path. The crystals grew hot and a smell of scorching leather rose from their feet.

"It's a trick, we are never going to reach anywhere" Maggie said, brushing away a beautiful crimson butterfly that had settled on her cheek. More butterflies fluttered around Josh and settled on his head and shoulders, their delicate wings tickling his skin. He ignored them and continued walking towards a thick curtain of plate-sized butterflies.

Maggie and Josh burst through the fluttering curtain and stepped into a large, vaulted room, ablaze with candles. It was filled with broken chairs, climbing frames and a long table littered with peanut shells. AJ stood before them, arms folded and clutching his wand. Stiltskins lined the wall behind him. Their tongues whipped and stitched the air. AJ's eyes darted directly to Maggie.

"I've been waiting for you," he said ominously.

"Everything is under control, Your Majesty," Maggie said, bowing. "Thanks to your guards and your faithful subjects, the rebellion and the two traitors will never be seen again."

"Good work, good work," AJ said. Josh winced beneath his visor, suddenly overwhelmed by a desire for one of Mrs Grubb's meals. His stomach rumbled.

"I'm thinking of nippin' over to the other side and bringin' the whole circus into the Kingdom, includin' that pesky Madam Lulu," AJ said. "I need more miners. There's so much Broken Magic these days and there's a big demand for it on the market, especially for jewellery and snuff boxes. Luckily, the old magicians are growin' weak, and the young ones aren't being taught the basics." He winked. "I'm not complainin'. It makes the mountains bigger, the miners busier, and me, richer, which makes me and my customers very, very happy." He offered Maggie a grape. She stepped towards him.

"That crown really suits you, Your Highness."

"Yes, it does," said AJ, visibly swelling. "I was born to be a king." His eyes narrowed. "Remember the good old days when we were playin' detective and looking for clues? I was dyin' to tell you but that would have scuppered things a bit. You didn't have a clue, did you?" He roared with spiteful laughter.

"No, you were very convincing as a detective and planting all those false clues."

Josh watched nervously as Maggie popped the grape into her mouth and moved closer to AJ.

"I was, wasn't I? But it's thanks to this little beauty that I am King." He kissed the wand and waved it in the air.

"It's like Brimstone's!"

"It *is* Brimstone's. He didn't know how to use it properly. This is what gets me in and out of the Kingdom. It's my key." Maggie and Josh eyed the wand with new interest.

"Every King needs soldiers and loyal subjects, but they often betray him," AJ said and shoved the wand under Maggie's nose, making her dizzy. "This little darlin' gives me the power to control everything and everyone. Get my drift?" He grabbed her hand and held it tightly. She was surprised by how strong his grip was. "You're cleverer than I thought, Miss Bird Angel, considerin' all wands look the same. But this is not just a two-a-penny wand. Oh no. This is the real thing. It's more powerful than the universe. That silly old fool, Brimstone, was too weak for it."

Maggie looked across at Josh who stood stiffly to attention before them. She held her breath. He stepped forward as if to seize the wand. The Stiltskins immediately stepped towards him with a metallic click. AJ's cold stare was interrupted by several monkeys entering the Hall dragging an undressed Bone Head behind them. They saluted their King and threw their captive forward.

"Who's that?" AJ demanded.

The Bone Head whimpered and clutched his head. "A miner attacked me, Your Majesty, and took my clothes. He's in the Kingdom somewhere pretending to be me and wearing my uniform."

Josh stepped forward. "We shall find him, Your Majesty."

"What did he look like?" AJ barked.

Josh's heart sank, as the Bone Head described him. Furious, AJ hopped from one leg to another. "Impossible. It's that boy at the circus, wots-'is-name, Josh. He was in the Room of Eatin' Darkness. No one escapes from there. They should be finished by now."

"It's impossible to escape from the Dark," Josh said.

AJ turned to him. "Organise an inspection parade and

get all the Bone Heads to take their helmets and visors off. We'll soon know who this traitor is."

Josh bowed and led the monkeys through the butterflies. Maggie attempted to follow, but AJ commanded her to stay. "Keep your ears to the ground. I'm sure the Bone Heads are in cahoots with this. They must have known there was an imposter in their midst. Find out who else is workin' with that boy. Report to me immediately. I shall make them all suffer." He waved her away. When she looked back, he was polishing his wand and whistling as if he did not have a care in the world.

25

Maggie sidled up to Brimstone. "AJ has your wand," she whispered. Brimstone glanced nervously around the Treasure Chamber before replying, "I know. He stole it from me and refused to give it back. He said it had always been his but because magic has been acting strangely, it went missing. He had to look for it because he couldn't be King without it and expand his empire. He's nothing without it. Don't go near him when he's got it in his hand. He's dangerous."

"If you had it back, do you think you could use it properly?"

Brimstone shrugged his shoulders. "I don't know. Maybe, if I tried…"

"We have to get it from him."

"He never lets go of it."

"Are you good at making plans, Brimstone?"

"I'm better at plans than I am at magic but plans take time, and, frankly, I don't think we have enough of it…"

He was interrupted by a group of shouting Bone Heads marching into the Chamber and pulling Josh behind them. His helmet and visor had been torn away, revealing his frightened face. The Voice announced the King and the Chamber fell silent.

AJ strutted in with his entourage of monkeys and guards. He leapt onto Josh's back, dug his fingers into his skin and snapped his teeth over his ear. "You have been unmasked," he hissed. "Those who betray their King must be punished. You shall not escape this time and your punishment shall be worse."

Leaping from Josh's back he swung round to face his Bone Heads. "You lot must have known he was an imposter. You hid him. Traitors the lot of you."

The Bone Heads chorused in protest and Josh looked frantically around the Chamber for Maggie. But she was nowhere to be seen. Who would rescue him now?

Maggie peered out from inside one of the large boxes stacked around the Chamber. They had only just found each other again, and now she was about to lose Josh forever. Her body tensed, ready to spring like a cat.

AJ pointed the wand at his Bone Heads. "I'll show you what your King does to traitors." He swung the wand in a wide circle around one of them. "North, South, East, West, take this traitor. Do your best," he chanted.

The Bone Head gave a loud scream, levitated, sparked and disappeared in a puff of smoke. A sudden blast of wind cleared the air, and he was gone. The Chamber fell into terrified silence.

"Who's next?" asked AJ, prodding the Bone Heads with his wand as he walked through them.

Wanting to look brave, Josh tried to stop himself from shaking. AJ turned to face him. This was the end.

"Hang on," AJ said, as if struck by a sudden thought. He pressed the wand into Josh's stomach. "I came to your gaff with a letter from Madam Lulu for you. You were at the Scribbens' school, and so was that Bird Angel before she hit the circus. She's your mate, isn't she? Where is she?"

He stared around at the miners. "Which one of you is hidin' her?"

Terrified, they lowered their eyes to their boots. Brimstone stepped forwards.

"I know where she is, Your Majesty."

Maggie tensed. Was Brimstone about to betray her?

"You useless pile of tired old magic, you don't know nuffin'," AJ screamed, ordering Brimstone to come closer. "Where's the brat?"

"Please allow me to whisper in your ear, Your Majesty," Brimstone said. "Such things must be kept secret. There are those amongst us who would spirit her away immediately and hide her from you."

"You're right. The Kingdom is full of narks, thieves and murderers. I can't trust no one," AJ said, squinting at the miners and pointing at them. "I'm your Master, *and* if any of you are found hidin' that Maggie girl, you'll never see daylight again."

A collective shudder passed through the Chamber. Brimstone moved within arm's length of AJ.

"Your crown is a bit lopsided, Your Majesty. It makes you look foolish," he said. AJ raised a free hand to his head. Brimstone's arm shot forwards and grabbed the wand.

AJ immediately tried to snatch it back. "Seize him!" he screamed at the Bone Heads. They ignored him. "Stiltskins get here, quick."

The Stiltskins threaded their tongues through their eyes and took wide steps towards the King. The miners stuck their feet out and tripped them over. They fell to the floor, stilts clinking on stone, tongues tangling in the air.

"Don't come near me," Brimstone said, brandishing the wand like a sword. "Or I'll turn you all to dust."

The Bone Heads shrank away, leaving Josh standing alone.

"Ignore him. He can't do anything," AJ sneered. "He's a lousy magician. The wand won't do anything he wants it to."

Brimstone looked nervously at the wand. AJ was right. He *was* the worst magician ever.

"Brimstone, you can do it," Josh urged. "You're the best. You know you're the best. Please."

Brimstone puffed his chest out like a pigeon and strutted towards a group of monkeys. They bared their teeth and growled. AJ roared with laughter. "Pathetic, Brimstone, pathetic."

With a will of its own, the wand spun in Brimstone's palm and yanked his arm upwards.

"Oh, mighty wand!" he shouted. "Give power to all that's good. Do what you must. Turn evil to dust."

The wand swooped down like a hawk, pulling his arm with it. Something shattered, like a mirror breaking, and a circle of tiny flames licked around the huddled monkeys. A thick wreath of smoke rose into the air. When it cleared, the monkeys had gone, replaced by small piles of dust.

The miners roared in disbelief and turned to each other in triumph.

AJ ran his hands disbelievingly through the ash. He looked up at Brimstone. "It's a trick," he screamed. "I'm still your Master. I'm your King. You do what I say."

He snatched at the wand, but Josh overpowered him. They fell crashing to the floor. The miners cheered and Josh tossed them the crown. The Bone Heads threw off their helmets and visors and danced. The monkeys fled into the tunnels. Muscles threw himself on a whimpering AJ and tore his royal cloak into strips. An incredulous silence

filled the Chamber as he wound them tightly around AJ's wrists and ankles.

Mrs Gumbo kissed Brimstone furiously on the cheeks and Tearful wept profusely in his arms; Fozia climbed laughing onto his shoulders. Maggie climbed out of the box and shouted over to Josh, "Let's go!"

He gave a broad grin, "You've missed all the excitement," he said, and beckoned to Brimstone.

The magician stared down at AJ with a mix of contempt and pity. "Look who's the idiot now, King of Nothing."

"We don't have time for this, Brimstone. The wand is the key and will get us out. You need to get it to turn the lock." Josh said.

AJ laughed loudly. "Fools."

Brimstone kissed the wand, and smiled. "I'll do my best."

"You can do it," Maggie said.

Brimstone nodded, but deep down his newfound confidence was draining away. What if turning the monkeys to dust was just a one-off and AJ was right – he really was a lousy magician?

Maggie hauled AJ to his feet. "You said the wand was your key to entering the Kingdom. Now you are going to show us how it lets you out."

AJ burst into hysterical laughter. "Turning monkeys to dust is one thing, using the wand to get you out of the Kingdom is another. Impossible."

"If you don't tell us where the exit is, we'll throw you into the Room of Eating Darkness," the miners yelled.

"Alright, alright," AJ said. "As long as you take me with you."

Maggie glanced at Josh. There was no way AJ could be allowed to leave the Kingdom, but they nodded in agreement. They would do anything to escape the Kingdom and its monarch, even lie.

"I'll take you there, but first, you'll have to untie me," AJ said,

"No way," Muscles said as he and Brimstone dragged him through the miners.

"Lead the way," Mrs Gumbo said, and AJ pointed towards the huge rusting door opening before them. They surged through the Waiting Room towards the place that had been the beginning of the Kingdom for them all.

26

Once more they stood beneath the flooded ceiling. Rabbits skipped around their feet and flocks of newly arrived birds fluttered above them, confused and afraid.

"This is where I arrived," Maggie said, looking around her.

Brimstone looked around him. "Me too."

"There was a pinprick of light behind me and I felt as if I'd been squeezed through it," said Yui. "All my muscles ached."

"It was so tiny, I don't understand how I could have fitted through it," Mrs Gumbo said. "Now, I'm like a skeleton. I could squeeze through easily." She looked angrily at AJ. "Tell us how to get out. You must know. You're always popping in and out of the Kingdom to sell your treasure and overseeing the invisible transportation of us slaves."

AJ struggled in Muscle's arms. "Untie me and I'll show you."

"Dream on, monkey," said Mrs Gumbo, balancing his crown on top of her turban and mimicking his voice.

"I wouldn't trust him with the wand," Maggie said. "Brimstone has to keep and use it."

"Me?" Brimstone cried, horrified. "What if I get it wrong, and we all end up being eaten by the Dark?"

"You've just done some great magic, and you can do it again and get us out."

Brimstone's moustache trembled. The miners shifted uneasily towards him.

"He can't do it," AJ sneered. Tearful coughed on a sob.

"We must find the exit," Maggie said. "If this was where we entered, it's probably where we leave."

"We'll never find it," Tearful wailed.

No one knows how long they searched for the

pinhole of light, but a huge cry of relief greeted Fozia's sudden shout of "I've found it!"

All heads turned to a barely perceptible glimmer of light. "It must be a sort of keyhole," she said as it shifted away from her and moved up towards the watery ceiling like a glittering insect.

"We'll lose it if it goes any higher," said Josh.

Brimstone took a deep breath and jabbed the wand into the point of light. The crowd gasped. He pulled at the wand. "It's stuck. I can't get it out."

"Give it a good tug," shouted Mrs Gumbo.

Brimstone stared up at the river flowing above him, and in a voice that didn't sound like his, boomed, "Oh bravest wand, whose power is strong, make this pinhole broad and long. Set us free and break our chains. Make us whole and send us home."

The light expanded into a halo around the wand. Excitement mounted. "It's getting bigger. We're going home!" Yui shouted, and everyone cheered. The birds dived and swooped above them while the light expanded to the size of a pancake and stopped. Brimstone tugged at the wand. It refused to budge. AJ sniggered. Muscles dropped him to the floor and he landed with a loud thud.

"We won't all fit through that," Mrs Gumbo sighed.

"I won't," Yui said. "Not with these legs."

"You have to make it bigger," Maggie said.

Brimstone repeated the incantation and blew on the wand, begging it to work. The wand wiggled and the light contracted.

"It's getting smaller," the crowd cried in despair.

"It's still stuck," Brimstone wailed. "I told you I'm the worst magician ever. What shall we do?"

AJ burst into mocking laughter. "We shall be here forever."

Tearful wailed that he wanted to see his brothers. As if given a signal, everyone suddenly chorused the names of those they loved and missed.

Josh's face brightened. "What about the stone? That might help," he said.

"A stone?" Brimstone said. "Don't be ridiculous!"

Maggie pressed her hand against the stone. It tick-tocked against her chest. How could she have forgotten it? She pulled it out and clenched it tightly in her hand. Closing her eyes, she imagined everyone as leaves blown across the sky by a great wind. Her cheeks puffed and she blew into the air. Josh stared at her, unaware of the stone warming and pulsing in her clenched hand.

"It's turning. The wand is turning!" Brimstone cried.

Maggie's breath grew deep and calm. She clasped the stone to her chest and it beat in time with her heart. An image of leaves floating to the earth rose before her. Brimstone repeated the incantation, but this time everyone joined in.

She heard a key turn in a lock and opened her eyes. The light had expanded into a large circle.

"I could get through that," Mrs Gumbo said, gathering her skirts, not noticing that the circle was slowly fading. Brimstone pulled hard at the wand. It still wouldn't budge.

"Idiots the lot of you," AJ said, struggling to free himself.

Maggie stepped back, gulped and aimed the stone at the faintly glimmering circle. It hit the centre and the wand shot out with a loud crack, sending Brimstone to the floor. A deafening explosion followed, and a galaxy of stars burst above them.

The scrape and rasp of iron against iron filled the Kingdom as an enormous dragon's head broke through the floor with a deafening crash. Clouds of scalding steam billowed from its glowing nostrils. Everyone looked on in terror as it rose above them. Iron spikes lined its spine and hissing pistons pulled at its limbs. It lowered its rusting head and opened its vast, fanged jaws A long metallic tongue shot from its mouth like a never-ending road and licked at the air. Its bright green eyes spun like speeding planets. The miners froze, not knowing where to run.

"The Iron Dragon!" shouted AJ, struggling to free himself.

Brimstone stood over him. "Is this rusty pile of tin going to get us out of here?"

"What else is there, stupid?"

The dragon's tongue snapped back and its colossal jaws lowered with a loud mechanical click.

"I think it wants to eat us," Josh said in a quaking voice.

Mrs Gumbo stared up at the creature with bright eyes. "It's wonderful. I would love to have a dragon for the circus. People would come for miles to watch it perform."

The dragon's head twisted and grated as its jaws winched open in a huge yawn. The miners clung fearfuly to each other as its eyelids rose and fell in a slow bored blink.

"Not again," it drawled in a voice that sounded like screeching brakes and chuffing trains. "I do have other things to do – like sleep. Lots of sleep."

The air dampened as clouds of steam blew from its nostrils. Its eyes rested on AJ. "Where do you want to go now? Just because you're King it doesn't mean I'm your taxi. Anyway, where's your crown?"

"He's not the King anymore," Josh shouted up to the dragon.

"Thank goodness for that. He wasn't a good one," the dragon said. "But who has the wand? He's nothing without the wand."

Brimstone stepped forwards and held out the wand. The dragon belched fire, and cogs and wheels whirred inside him. "Well done," he chuffed.

"Please sir, can you take us out of the Kingdom?" asked Maggie.

"Do you have a return ticket?"

Maggie shook her head.

"It's impossible. You have to have a return ticket."

"We don't need a return, just one-way. We're not coming back."

"Not coming back? You mean, you just want me to take you OUT of the Kingdom forever?"

Everyone nodded their heads.

"In that case you don't need a ticket. I don't want to come back either," said the Iron Dragon, tilting his head towards AJ. "He's not coming as well, is he?"

"No," said Maggie.

"Even better," said the dragon with what could have been a smile. "He never gives a tip and just leaves me to rust. No wonder I'm so tired all the time. If I continue rusting, there'll be nothing of me left."

"Which is why you must leave – with us," Josh said.

The dragon lowered his body towards them. "Yes, I could have a good clean and get my cogs oiled." He flipped his tail and looked over the crowd. "My goodness, there's an awful lot of you. I can't take all of you. Some of you will have to stay behind."

"Impossible," Maggie said. "You're big enough to take us all."

"It's not about room. It's about weight. I might not be able to lift off."

"We can try. I'm sure you can do it," Josh said.

"Years of neglect won't make it easy," the dragon said, looking pointedly at AJ.

"I'm coming with you," AJ said. "You said I could."

Maggie turned to the miners. "Can he?"

Their response was immediate and unanimous: "No!"

The dragon roared belching fire. AJ's fur stood on end, his tail twitched. "I promise I'll be good."

Josh shook his head. AJ pleaded. "I'm a top juggler. The circus needs a juggler."

"Jugglers are two–a–penny," Mrs Gumbo said, thrusting

her face into his. "You can stay in your little Kingdom and play with your Broken Magic."

"You wait, I'll get my revenge. Don't think magic can be mended overnight. It needs a King like me to fix it. I'm the most powerful magician in the world and one day I will be the King of Everything."

"Not without this, you won't," Brimstone said, tapping the wand in his pocket with a satisfied smile.

The dragon clanked its tail impatiently and steam rose in the air. Birds flew into its waiting mouth. The miners and Bone Heads surged forwards. Grabbing rabbits, snakes and kittens they swarmed over the dragon's body, chanting, "Miners no more!"

"Don't leave me!" AJ screamed.

Maggie and Josh looked back at him; without his crown and cloak he looked pathetic. Josh took a step towards him.

"Leave him, Josh," Maggie said. "If we take him with us, he will magic us back into the Kingdom again and throw you into the Room again."

"Maybe he didn't mean it," Josh said as AJ shot him a pleading look.

"Of course he did. Don't be silly. He'll be OK here with his treasure and his monkeys to keep him company,"

Maggie said, waving a cheerful goodbye to AJ. "We have to go, Josh, or we'll be left behind with him."

Cylinders fired from within the dragon's belly, pistons cranked and its innards whirred and clattered like the workings of an old rusted clock. Gears and cogs groaned and creaked as they worked to open its webbed iron wings into enormous sails. It straightened its spine while its passengers clung to anything they could. Birds perched on shoulders; rabbits, mice and kittens settled in laps and pockets; snakes curled around legs.

Maggie pulled Josh towards the dragon, but he refused to move. "I'm not going," he said.

"Are you mad? You can't stay with AJ!"

"What if it's all a trick, and the Iron Dragon's going to take us somewhere worse than any Room?"

"Don't be ridiculous. If you stay here, AJ will throw you into one. You have to trust the magic," Maggie said, tugging urgently at him.

"What has magic done for us – nothing. It's made us slaves of AJ. And now we could be slaves to this monster," Josh said. They both looked at the dragon, who stared back at them with wise, sorrowful eyes.

"I think it's a lot nicer than AJ," Maggie said. "And anyway, it was the wand and the stone that provided the magic, not AJ. You have to trust the magic, Josh. It's not broken anymore."

She looked behind her. AJ had freed himself and was running towards the dragon with a crowd of snarling monkeys. "We're coming with you!" he shouted. "You can't forget your best mate."

"Quick Josh, we have to go," Maggie screamed. Josh stood transfixed as AJ headed towards them.

"I can't move," he said.

Maggie yanked him forwards. AJ and the monkeys grew nearer. She looked back at the dragon preparing to leave. Brimstone and Muscles hung from its mouth, reaching out to them. "We don't have time to wait. Hurry!" they shouted.

There was a sudden whoosh, and a deluge of playing cards sliced through the air. AJ and the monkeys ran squealing for cover. Cards bounced off the dragon as its wings cantilevered out, releasing flakes of rust that swirled around in thick clouds. Maggie pushed Josh forwards, gripped his hand and pulled him towards the dragon's gaping jaws. Cards bounced off her back as she grabbed Muscles' hand. A Four of Clubs stabbed Josh's hand. He let out a loud cry and fell sprawling to the floor. Maggie reached down, one hand still holding tight onto Muscles, and urged Josh to take her wrist. Muscles held on to her while Josh grabbed at her hand and swung unsteadily from her arm. Steam billowed from the dragon's body as it levered itself into an upright position.

"Ready for lift off," it said as Maggie and Josh hung from its mouth like shreds of meat. Its chest heaved and chugged noisily like a steam train. Muscles flexed his arms and pulled them both into the dragon.

"That was close," Josh said, thanking his rescuers. He turned to Maggie. "I didn't know you were so strong."

She picked an Ace of Hearts from his hair and flexed her wrists proudly. "I'm the one-and-only Bird Angel," she said with a wink.

The dragon's head pushed through the river and a tsunami roared through the Kingdom, taking everything with it. Maggie looked down. AJ had disappeared. The miners watched silently as the Kingdom of Broken Magic sealed itself behind them and vanished, as if it had never existed.

Maggie clung tightly to the dragon and gazed spellbound into an endless sea of darkness. "We did it Josh. We've escaped for good, and we didn't even have a Plan."

"I wish we had a Plan for a nice plate of pie with peas

and onions and gravy," Josh said, licking his lips and wondering if the dragon provided meals.

"I just want to smell sawdust and Madam Lulu's perfume," Maggie said, wondering if Josh was right and this might all be a trick and they would never see the circus, or anything else, ever again. The dragon settled into a steady flight, its inner engines hissing and hammering. A meteorite sped past them and, as if given a signal, the creature sped forwards and tore through the universe. Its passengers watched spellbound as stars birthed and died around them and new and ancient earths spun and shone in countless galaxies. Strange, unworldly music played in their ears. Hypnotised by the beauty of the new world, Maggie's eyes grew heavy. The dragon's warm breath rose and fell, lulling its passengers into a quiet calm. Soon everyone was asleep, until a sudden clanking and clanging from deep within the creature's belly shook them awake. They clung to the quaking dragon in terror.

"I think it's going to be sick," Brimstone said.

"Oh no!" Mrs Gumbo screamed as the dragon gave a huge belch and a great wind surged around them. Fire and sparks burst from its nostrils with a mighty judder. A hot blast of foul-smelling steam broke from the back of its throat like a hurricane. It shook and spat its passengers out into the cosmos with a rattling snort.

"Pardon me," it said as they fell screaming into nothingness. Nobody saw the Iron Dragon sail on through the cosmos. They could only remember swirling like crumbs through clouds before losing consciousness. All around the world, people looked up to see their lost loved ones drifting gently towards them and landing at their feet.

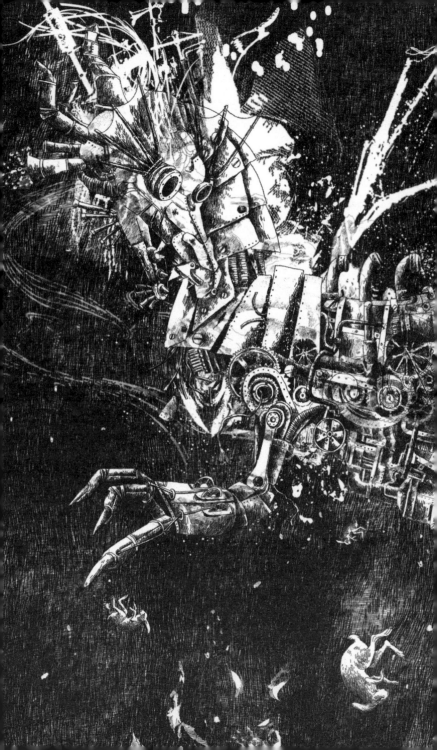

27

Maggie and Josh landed with a bump outside the Big Top. Brimstone, Mrs Gumbo and Tearful lay sprawled on their backs beside them. Fozia and the three girls floated over the caravans before landing by the ticket booth. Josh sat up, covered in flakes of rust, the hiss of steam still echoing in his ears. He pulled Maggie to her feet. Madam Lulu and Mr Banerjee rushed joyfully towards them with open arms. The tigers whooped and danced in welcome. McTavish wound long, knitted scarves around their necks: "To keep you warm, for winter."

Maggie rubbed her eyes. "How long have we been away for?"

Madam Lulu shook her head. "A week I think, though it feels much, much longer."

"A week?" Josh said, shivering in the cold. "Is it still winter?"

"It's a strange business altogether," Mr Banerjee said vaguely.

"We have such a lot to tell you all," Josh said. "But you'll never believe us."

Maggie eyed Mr Banerjee. Hadn't she seen him somewhere before?

Soon everyone was seated in the circus ring around a long table, holding hands. The air was full of laughter and kisses. Tearful sat beside his brothers, weeping with what he said was happiness. Brimstone strolled up and down to make sure everyone admired his newly waxed moustache. Mrs Gumbo sat at the head of the table, AJ's crown perched upon her turban. She glanced across at Yui and Muscles. "What are you both doing here? You belong to another circus."

Yui smiled and proudly crossed her elegant, returned legs. "We wanted to be with you, so we were dropped here."

"I have my legs back so I can still perform," Muscles said, proudly lifting a hairy, muscled leg that was once belonged to Yui. "I bet you miss them."

"I do – sometimes, Yui said.

Mrs Gumbo stood, whacked a spoon on the table and laughed. "Can you juggle?"

"Yes, and more," they chorused.

"Good. You can replace that horrible monkey. He wasn't a very good juggler anyway," Mrs Gumbo said, holding out her arms. "Welcome to the greatest show on earth, Mrs Gumbo's Flying Circus."

The tigers roared and everyone clapped, stomped feet and paws, and cheered.

Over a hot and delicious meal, amidst gasps and low mutterings, Maggie revealed the truth of AJ and the Kingdom of Broken Magic.

"How utterly dreadful," Madam Lulu cried, crushing Maggie to her glittering chest. "Once you start performing, my darling angel, you shall forget this dreadful time, and we have Fozia, Aisha, Alice and Loka with us now. We shall make a wonderful flying team."

The four girls picked nervously at their food. "I don't think we're ready, Madam Lulu. It's been a long time," they said.

"Practise, practise, practise my dears. It's like riding a bike. You never forget."

"And how did you get out of that dreadful place?" Mr Banerjee asked.

"I'm such a pathetic magician, we nearly didn't," Brimstone said, pulling the wand from his pocket and waving it in the air.

"Put it back, Brimstone, you never know what it will do," Mrs Gumbo said. "We don't want to go back to the Kingdom."

"There are thousands of magic wands around the world, but this one is particularly powerful," Brimstone said. "AJ used it to suck magic from all the others, so that they became weak. A wand depends on the intention of its user. He had a huge hunger for power and wealth. He didn't care how he got it and used the wand to help him."

"Without you, we would have never escaped," Maggie said. "You opened the circle of light and awakened the Iron Dragon. You're a great magician."

Brimstone blushed and preened his moustache. "Thank you, but without the stone, the dragon would never have appeared."

Maggie pressed her hand against her chest. The stone wasn't there! She searched through her clothes.

"It's gone. I've lost the stone and I've got to give it back!" she cried.

"Never mind," Mr Banerjee said.

Maggie jumped out of her chair in a sudden shock of

recognition. "You're the gentleman I stole it from," she said shamefacedly. He smiled and reached into his jacket's top pocket. The stone blinked at her from the palm of his hand. Dumbstruck, Maggie fell back into her chair.

"How did it get there, sir?" Josh asked, astonished.

"There's more to magic than you know," Mr Banerjee said mysteriously as he tucked the stone back into his pocket.

In the evening, the circus gathered round a great fire. The tigers drummed and sang while Maggie and Josh snuggled into their fur. Behind them, McTavish's knitting needles clicked and clacked in time to the drumming. Yui showed off her fire-eating skills while Muscles whirled heavy soup tureens on sticks, his muscles rippling like stones in his arms. Brimstone sat beside Mr Banerjee. Both men stared thoughtfully into the fire, ignoring the parrots and doves perching upon them and the rabbits nibbling their shoe laces. Fozia and Alice lay sleeping in Mrs Gumbo's arms while Aisha and Loka lay beside her under blankets.

"Mr Banerjee wants me to stay with him," Josh said, poking the fire with a stick. "He wants to send me to school."

"Madam Lulu wants me to stay with the circus," Maggie said. Sparks flew around them as they struggled to say what they had always feared the most. Josh finally broke the silence. "It means we won't be together anymore, Mags." He threw the stick into the fire and hid his head in his hands.

"We can't go back to the Home," Maggie said.

"The Home is gone. Mr Banerjee is going to turn it into a proper school and orphanage for the children and he wants me to live with him and Mrs Grubb. You should see the house, Mags; it's huge and the food is everything we always dreamed about. Dinner is served every day, and there's lunch and breakfast too!"

Maggie squeezed his hand. "You have to go, Josh. You'll get a good education and everything you ever wanted. Mr Banerjee is a kind man and he's lonely. You'll be a good son to him. Besides, he has the stone." She winked and Josh grinned.

"I'm sure Mr Banerjee wouldn't mind if you came too, Mags."

Maggie shook her head. "I belong here, with Madam Lulu. The circus is my family. You saw me performing. It's what I was born to do. It's my future. Yours, Josh, is to become an educated gentleman like Mr Banerjee,"

They looked across at Mr Banerjee and Madam Lulu waving and smiling at them.

"We've found our families, haven't we?" Maggie said.

"Yes. It's what we've always dreamed of. Remember? But even when we're apart we can still be close," Josh said, putting an arm around Maggie's shoulder. "We can visit each other, and still have adventures."

"When are you and Mr Banerjee leaving?"

"Tomorrow," Josh said, squeezing Maggie so hard she thought her bones might break. She buried her head in his shoulders to hide her sadness.

"We'll see each other soon," Josh said, trying to sound cheerful. "Mr Banerjee has asked the circus to perform for the Home."

"C'mon you two, don't be miserable. Let's dance," Rara said, holding out her paws. They jumped up and sang and danced until dew jewelled the grass and the fire's embers grew cold.

Maggie didn't recognise the Scribbens' Home for Very Wayward Children. Its windows sparkled in the sunlight and its bricks glowed a warm red. The gates and doors were newly painted, and trees grew in the forecourt. Above the main entrance, a large sign announced The Banerjee School for Boys and Girls. Mr Banerjee and Josh came out to greet the circus and watched as horses were unhitched and caravans pitched. Tents sprouted like mushrooms around the school while the crew heaved huge rolls of canvas over the Big Top's central pole. Josh helped lift boxes from the wagons and Maggie thought how much he had changed. He was not the thin, scabby boy she had once known. He was now a well-dressed young gentleman but still with his happy grin and teasing banter. Children poured from the building and surrounded her. Their faces shone at the pleasure of seeing her again. Maggie complimented them on their tailored uniforms and polished shoes. "Miss Scribbens and Carry-On have gone!" they cheered. A girl tugged at her hand. "We can tell the difference between one end of a pen from another now, and how to dip it in ink and write words. It's like magic. And we can eat all we want," she said.

"Is it true you can fly, Maggie?" another child asked. She nodded her head and smiled, pushing back memories of cruel and dreadful times.

"Let's help get the circus ready," Mr Banerjee said.

By the evening the Big Top was filled with excited children. Maggie watched them laugh and cheer through the acts, except for the Grizzling Brothers. Soon it would be her turn. She pressed her hand nervously against her chest. She didn't have the stone anymore. Would she still be able to fly? Madam Lulu scolded her, "Of course you will. You're going to give your best performance ever for Josh and all your friends."

The tigers growled in agreement and flicked their tails. "Show 'em girl," Rara said. The Grizzling Brothers blew into their handkerchiefs and sobbed, "You'll be the best ever."

"We're going to walk the tightrope, and do a few somersaults," Fozia said. "But you are going to be the star, Maggie."

"You're on after Brimstone," McTavish said. The magician smiled nervously. Mrs Gumbo winked at him. "Your magic made mistakes because you didn't believe in yourself. You didn't think you were good enough and that you were too old. But a wand will only be as good as you think you are. And you're a good man."

"You're right, I am," Brimstone said, preening his moustache and stepping confidently into the ring. The children roared. He raised his top hat with a flourish and bowed. He tapped it with the wand and it shot into the air, releasing hundreds of flowers that fell like rain. He performed one perfect magic trick after another: rainbows poured from hats and handbags, fobs flew from pockets and exploded into bolts of thunder and lightning before returning to their owners, pigeons disappeared from beneath silk handkerchiefs, and reappeared in the laps of matrons, several pupils levitated from their seats. He left the ring to deafening applause. "There's no Broken Magic anymore. Nobody and nothing has disappeared, or ever will," he said, turning triumphantly to Maggie.

The flames of the torches blazed around her as she stepped into the ring and the audience leaned eagerly towards her. Josh and Mr Banerjee waved at her as she clambered up the rope to the platform. Seconds later she was hanging upside down from her trapeze, her knees hooked over the bar, and looking down upon the expectant faces below her. A rush of adrenaline flooded her body and she realised how alive she felt in the air – much more than when she was on the ground. Madam Lulu swung towards her with outstretched arms. Maggie grabbed at her wrists and released her legs from the bar. The crowd gasped as she hung from Madam Lulu's arms. Josh whistled loudly and Mr Banerjee threw his cane into the air. Madam Lulu swung backwards and forwards, faster and faster, until Maggie suddenly released herself, corkscrewed into the air and flew at great speed through a series of burning hoops.

"This is just the beginning," she shouted as she dive-bombed her audience and the Big Top trembled.

About the author

Christine Aziz has worked as a freelance journalist for almost thirty years. Her focus has been on reporting on the lives of women in conflict areas, particularly Afghanistan, the Middle East and Africa. Her debut novel, *The Olive Readers*, was selected from more than 46,000 entries to the Channel 4 How to Get Published Competition with Richard and Judy. She is a published poet, and several of her plays, monologues and an opera have been performed and staged in the UK. She is a creative writing tutor at the Arts University, Bournemouth and has held creative community workshops for children and young adults in Egypt, Morocco and the UK. This is her first book for children.